AVENGED

JUSTIN WRIGHT SUSPENSE SERIES
BOOK 3

ROB KAUFMAN

Avenged

Copyright © 2023 by Rob Kaufman

For the man who brought me into this world,
has consistently kept me on track, and continues to show me
there's always a light at the end of the tunnel. . .
no matter how dark things may seem.

PROLOGUE

J ustin threw open the front door and stormed into his home. He tossed his keys into the bowl on the console table and glanced around the adjoining rooms, searching, on guard.

Mandy met him as he stomped into the living room. She put her arms around him and kissed his cheek.

"You're trembling," she said. "Do you feel okay? It's still almost seventy degrees out there. You shouldn't be shaking like a leaf when the temperature is —"

"Where's Michael?"

"He's not here, and I'm really starting to worry. . . or get angry. I'm not sure yet," she said, taking a few steps back. "Tell me what's going on? What happened tonight?"

Justin dropped onto the sofa, but an instant later, he jumped up to pace. Wringing his hands, he went to the windows and looked into the backyard. The sun had set on the summer day some hours ago, leaving nothing to see. So he returned to the living room, where he circled the couch.

"Justin, stop!" Mandy shouted, standing in front of him so he'd stop walking. "Please slow down for a second and tell me what's going on."

She held his arms and, when he tried to get free of her, tightened her grip.

"I just came from the hospital," he said.

"That much I know," she replied. "I was waiting for you to call me and tell me you were on your way home."

"I couldn't call. Couldn't talk. I was. . ." He blew out a breath. "*Way* too angry and confused."

"Oh, and now you're so calm and levelheaded? Justin, what the hell is going on?"

He looked around again. "Why isn't Michael home? It's almost eleven o'clock. You let him go out after what he pulled today? Is he seeing that guy Anthony again? Or someone else? Where the hell is he?"

"Whoa," Mandy said. She pulled his arms, trying to bring him back to the sofa. "First, please tell me what happened at Bellevue. You once said your patient had never been very open or cooperative. Did she totally shut down, or did she *say* something to make you this angry?"

He combed his fingers through his hair and took a deep breath. "I saw that piece of shit, Devlin."

Knowing how much it would upset her, he hadn't planned to say anything about the encounter at Bellevue. But even after the trip home, his emotions were too raw to keep what happened at the hospital inside. And he realized that stomping around their house without an explanation wouldn't be any kinder to his wife.

Mandy fell back against the sofa cushions. "Oh my God. Not *him*! I thought you went to see that woman, your patient, the one that Parsons — "

"I did. We met and talked. And that's just another thing I have to contend with. But right now, Michael comes first."

He sat down on the couch again, and this time he made himself stay there. Mandy placed her hand on his.

"What about Michael?" she asked, anxiety making her voice unsteady. "Does it have something to do with Devlin? What did he say to you?"

Justin tried to avoid meeting her eyes, not wanting to see the expression on Mandy's face when he told her about his confrontation with their son's murderer. But now she said, "Please, Justin, look at me and tell me what happened."

Justin put his other hand on top of hers. Okay, he'd tell it quickly. Like ripping off a Band-Aid — except in this case, it was more like tearing out the stitches on an unhealed wound. But there was no way around it. He knew Mandy wouldn't let him keep it inside any longer, even if he'd been able to.

"I was so close to leaving without seeing him. I was in the elevator, and the doors were closing. . . "

For a few seconds he couldn't take a breath. He closed his eyes and willed his heart to beat slower, softer.

"Then what?" Mandy pushed.

"Then they stopped. He had his arm against one of them, and he just stood there, looking at me with a smirk on. . . that face. The same face he had the night. . . the night. . . "

"I know, honey." Her voice was thick with tears. "I know the night you're talking about. Then what happened? He said something to you?"

Justin had thought about the conversation with Devlin the entire way home. He didn't know how seriously to take that bastard's threat, or his supposed gratitude to Michael, but the memory of his smug, ugly face made him want to strike out at something, someone, anything. Talking about that memory aloud, making it real to Mandy, to himself, here in the heart of their home...

He opened his eyes, looked at his wife, and tore out the bloody stitches holding their world together.

"He wanted me to thank Michael," Justin muttered.

"What?" Mandy's shoulders jolted as if an electric shock had run through them.

"He wanted me to thank Michael," he repeated more loudly, if not much more steadily.

"For what?"

He squeezed her hand. "He said, 'for taking care of Malone.'"

Mandy let go of Justin's hand and leaned back. Her face was drained of color, her eyes blankly staring at the other side of the room.

"Then he said that Berny was his first obstacle and there was one more to go... me."

A tear rolled down Mandy's cheek. Justin gently wiped it from her face.

"What do you think?" she asked finally, after a deliberate breath. "Is he telling the truth or inventing stories to make you think our son is a murderer?"

Justin shook his head. "I have to be honest. I just don't know. That's why I need to speak with Michael. We need some damn answers."

Mandy wiped her eyes. "I kept hoping," she said. "Once he returned to us and then Van Sessler recommended Lauren to you. . . I hoped if we just gave him time, that it would get better. That he'd really come back, that little boy we lost seven years ago. I don't know if it's possible anymore. Do you?"

"I do," Justin said. "I really do." He leaned his elbows on his knees, the weariness of the last two nights coming over him. "I just have to find out one thing first."

"Just one?" she asked, a little sarcastically.

"Well, it's important," he said with equal dryness. But when he met her gaze again, what he had to say was utterly serious.

"Does our son want to love me or kill me?"

CHAPTER 1

Richard Davis hated everyone.

He walked up Park Avenue, doing his best to avoid looking at the individual faces of the mob passing him on either side, marching zombies taking up more space than they needed on such a narrow sidewalk. The real problem was, despite his fervent attempt to dodge the glances, a zombie or two would somehow meet his eyes, setting off a loathing in his gut that welled up like poison in a boiling cauldron.

It didn't matter who — a pretty young woman flinging her hair into the face of the Con Edison worker behind her, a little boy holding his mother's hand for dear life, or a corporate suit with a phone so close to his mouth he looked on the verge of swallowing it. Adult or child, busy with purpose or idly wandering, smiling or scowling. Whoever it was, Richard couldn't help but feel sick, nauseated by the simple fact that these people were breathing.

The ones wearing sunglasses, he surmised, used the darkest lenses possible to hide their own hatred of the soulless robots around them.

And so many of the others, the ones without lenses hiding their revulsion, stared blankly forward as though nothing or no one else existed. Many of them held an expression of disgust — confidently indifferent to anyone who might recognize their disdain toward the human mass packing the streets.

Or was this all in his head? Was *he* the only person who felt this way — projecting his feelings onto others like a horror movie on a dingy theater screen? Or was it the truth? Did everyone hate everyone else, and that's how the world was?

Yeah, he thought, *no doubt. This is definitely how the world is.*

When he reached 45th Street, he surrendered to imitation and slipped on the sunglasses that had hung off his shirt collar since he'd left home. He didn't care when the sun suddenly snuck behind a gathering of thick gray-white cumulus clouds or that the heat and sweat from his cheeks fogged up his lenses. Anything was better than seeing people without a shield. And as fragile as this buffer was, the sunglasses made it easier for him to hide his animosity.

His tension grew as he neared Justin Wright's office. He was counting on a meeting with this "psychiatric magician" — as the doctor had been described in a recent *New York Times* article Richard read about anxiety — to help decrease his anger and hostility toward strangers.

He knew the origin of his negative feelings, but found it impossible to tame them. In due time, he'd tell Wright where and when they started, how one event lit a fire inside of him that burned every second of every day. But first he'd give this wizard of psychiatry a few sessions to work his magic, if he could.

Would he actually be able to help him control the red-hot seething inside? If even a glimmer appeared at the end of the tunnel, he'd continue his sessions and learn everything he could from Wright before ending their relationship in a way that would make him feel even better. But if the tunnel exit remained as dark and gloomy as it was right now, that meant he'd have to end things much sooner.

The phone in his front pants pocket started vibrating. Richard sighed as the pit of his stomach tightened. Knowing who it was, he had to take a breath before answering so he wouldn't lose his shit. . . and his job.

"Hello," he said.

"Hey, Richard. I need you for a four o'clock."

He glanced at his wristwatch and sighed again.

"Paul, it's almost three o'clock. I already told you I had an appointment from three to four. I can't make it."

"Yeah, I know, I know. But I can't track down Myles, and everyone else is busy."

"Dude, you'll have to do it yourself. I can't miss this meeting."

Silence. Ominous silence. Richard pictured Paul's snarl, his upper lip raised and baring his two pointy incisors, a vampiric appearance that took over when the man's anger confiscated his ability to speak.

"Are you still there?" Richard asked, pushing his own rage down.

"Yeah, yeah. I'm still here. Man, you'd better be on your way to a doctor because you have some deadly disease. You're really screwing me over here."

Richard pushed the phone harder against his ear to keep himself from hurling it onto the pavement.

"Damn it, Paul. I told you about this a week ago and reminded you yesterday *and* after my gig this morning. Do I have to do a fucking song and dance on your desk to get the message through? I mean, seriously, I don't know — "

"Watch your tone, Richie Boy. It's not like you're the only person who can do what you do. I can get someone — "

"Well, apparently, I *am* the only person, because you just said you can't find anyone."

Paul's next silent pause, even longer than the first, sent electrified tingles up the back of Richard's neck. He wasn't sure which one of them was more of a ticking time bomb, but un-fucking-fortunately, Paul was the boss, which gave him the upper hand. He'd pissed the guy off, and if he didn't make things right within the next few seconds, he could be looking for a job at 4:01.

"Listen, Paul. I'll be done by four o'clock. I'm available after that. I'll even work tonight if you need me to."

Paul's sigh was like a flood of air being released from a Macy's Thanksgiving Day parade balloon. *Jesus, you'd think I just told him his cocker spaniel got run over by a truck.* The thought made Richard smirk. *If only...*

"Okay, I'm holding you to it. I was going to take a six o'clock gig, but you can take it instead. I'll enjoy dinner at a normal hour for a change. Be here by twenty after five. Any later, and you'll be wishing your disease *was* fatal."

The line went dead. Richard slid the phone back into his pocket.

"You little fucker," he said, looking around for a trash can or hot dog vendor cart to kick. Even a homeless guy would do. The mass of zombies marched on, and as he made his way through them to the corner of 49th, the traffic light changed from red to green. *Damn it!* Now more people were crossing over Park to his left, surging like a tidal wave. His anger turned to fear and then threatened to become panic. He broke into a run, crossing 49th as a cab sped through the yellow light.

Tires screeched. Richard closed his eyes, waiting for the impact. But he didn't feel a thing, and he heard nothing but ringing in his ears and the shouting of the cab driver. When he opened his eyes, the cab's grill growled only inches from his left hip. One foot farther and he would've been smeared across the street, bones shattered.

The cabbie's screams persisted in a language Richard didn't understand. But, like the passersby who completely ignored his near-death experience, he did the same to the cab driver and paid his words no attention. He was safe, and his body was intact. Not that *one* of the thousands of people walking past him gave a shit, or at least pretended to. *Yeah, this is definitely the way the world is,* he grumbled inside and out.

He resumed his run toward 50th, where he turned right and then leaned against the wall of the building in which Justin Wright was probably waiting for him.

According to his watch, it was 2:58. Two minutes to spare. And to refill his lungs.

He took a few extra-deep breaths, stretched his neck, and shook his limbs to release some tension. There was no way he could let Justin Wright see him in panic mode. He had to be angry and irritated, not scared. If there was one thing Richard would not allow Dr. Wright to witness, it was fear.

CHAPTER 2

"Mandy, we have to get to the bottom of this." Outside Justin's office window, clouds rolled in above the Park Avenue skyscrapers. "We need to have a sit-down with Michael tonight. It's the only way we'll know whether or not to believe Devlin."

Her voice crackled through his speakerphone. "You mean that *thing* who murdered our son? We should let him make us wonder if Michael is a killer? I can't believe you would even consider — "

"I'm not considering anything. . ." He took a breath. "I just have a lot of questions and think we're both so close to the situation that our judgment is clouded. And since we can't talk to anyone else right now, in case Michael. . ." He paused, wanting to avoid making Mandy angrier. "In case Michael did something that could get him in trouble."

A few seconds passed. Justin turned to the phone and leaned with his elbows on his desk. He covered his face with his hands.

"I'll repeat what I said last week after your absurd question about whether Michael wants to love you or kill you. Yes, our boy has problems. And yes, I also have concerns. But not to the point where I think he'd hurt someone or where I'd let a psychopath like Devlin make me doubt my own son's stability. Please, Justin, I know the impact that man has had on our life, but you can't allow him to affect your judgment. Once that happens, we're on our way down a rabbit hole we may never get out of."

She was right. He knew that. But it was like the essence of Devlin had been infused into his bloodstream, giving him ideas he knew he should ignore and making him feel things that went against the logic on which he'd always prided himself.

"What about Katy?" Mandy asked. "If we talk with her about it, I think we can trust her to keep it under wraps. She's a detective, an investigator, for God's sake. She knows what to look for and how to find it. Yes, it's true Michael hasn't been speaking to us about important things, but we can't base our suspicions on a comment from some maniac. I think we should bring her in on this."

"Not yet," Justin insisted. "First, we talk with Michael and see if he tells us anything that might help clear things up. You're right; Devlin could be playing me, trying to get me bent out of shape by having me think Michael killed Berny. He's definitely sociopathic enough to do something like that."

"He's a pathetic murderer locked up in a psych unit." Mandy's voice trembled. "I don't trust a word that comes out of his mouth."

"I hear you, honey. I do. And I feel the same way. I mean, we're talking about our son."

"The other thing I have to do," he continued, "is check the logs and see who's been visiting Devlin, if anyone."

"Why? Do you expect to find Michael's name in those logs? I mean — you really think you're going to find your son's name in a book that has anything to do with that hospital?"

Emotions were high on both ends of the phone, and Justin couldn't let them escalate. He swallowed his frustration and cleared his throat.

"No, I don't think that. Not at all. Especially since I'm sure they would have notified me if he, or any minor, tried to visit Devlin." He took a breath. "I just want to check out every angle I possibly can to make sure I'm not missing anything."

"Okay, fine," she murmured, her doubt in his explanation coming through crystal clear. "Find out what you have to find out. But for the record, I'm telling you I believe our son is innocent, and Frank Devlin is screwing with you and our family... again. For some insane reason, your suffering brings him joy. And now he creates that suffering by saying just a few words. Please, Justin. You're too good a psychiatrist to fall for his crap."

He opened his mouth to respond but stopped before a sound could escape. Even though she'd also lost a son, a piece of her heart torn out to leave a fissure that would never close, she wasn't there when it happened. She didn't see the pain in Dylan's face, or hear the sound of his body collapsing onto the floor. She hadn't looked into the fear in his eyes as he took his last breath. Justin would never describe it to her, nor would he ever blame her for not understanding the chaos Devlin's presence created inside his head. She had enough demons of her own to deal with. He wouldn't add another one.

"You're right, Mandy. I know you're right. I think with everything this guy has done to us, I'm having some real problems working it through my head professionally. It goes too deep. It's in my veins, and I can't seem to treat it as I would a patient going through the same thing. Does that make any kind of sense?"

"Of course it does," she replied. "I'm sorry. Really, I am. I just. . . I don't know the right word to use. . . torn? The Michael I knew seven years ago wouldn't hurt a fly. And I can't believe he'd hurt one now. Am I deceiving myself? I don't know, and that's why I get so angry and confused. I want answers just like you. And I want them as soon as possible. And I think Katy can help us."

"Just a few more days, I promise. Let's talk to Michael and get his side of what's going on. Then we can bring Katy in to help us find out what Devlin is up to. Okay?" He waited for her to respond. She didn't. "Are you with me?"

"I'm always with you," she said. "I don't always agree with you, but I'm with you."

The bell outside Justin's office rang. He took Mandy off speaker and picked up the receiver.

"I know you are," he said. "Gotta go. New patient session. Be home around sevenish. Love you."

"And I you."

* * *

Justin waited for Richard Davis to take a seat before sitting across from him and setting his journal, along with Richard's paperwork, on his lap.

Something about the young man seemed familiar. Like he'd spotted him on the Rye-bound train or passed him on the street on his way to Johnny's Deli for lunch. Justin couldn't pinpoint the spot, but there was something —

"You're looking at me kind of funny," Richard said. "What's up with that?"

"I'm sorry. It's just that you look so familiar. I apologize if the answer is yes and I'm not remembering, but have we met before?"

Richard shook his head and offered a faint smile. "Not that I'm aware of," he said. "There's no reason to apologize."

Justin closed his eyes for a second, trying to come up with where he might've seen this man before. A courthouse before testifying? A prison cell? The interrogation room at the police station?

Wow, has my life come to this? The only place I might have previously seen a familiar face is inside the criminal justice system?

He tried to remember something, anything else — An APA event? The subway? — but came up with nothing.

"Okay. Who knows? Maybe you look like someone I see on the train all the time. Or someone I saw at a lecture..." He stopped talking and cleared his throat. "I'm sorry. I got us off track — no pun intended."

"No problem. You sound like a very busy man," Richard said.

"Not too busy to read the information you provided about yourself. I see you live close by, so it's pretty easy for you to get here if you're coming from home."

"Yeah," Richard said. "I used to live downtown, but my girlfriend got a great new job, and we 'moved on up.' She's also making a lot more money, which helps pay for these sessions."

Talking money with patients had always been a sensitive issue for Justin. It immediately took the focus off the topic at hand and brought it to the pocketbook, a place where many patients would dwell if not "cured" within a few sessions.

"What does she do?"

"Marketing for some mid-size company."

"And what do *you* do?" Justin asked, glancing down at the paper on top of the pile. "It says here you're in the auto industry."

"Transport, actually. Getting cars and people from one place to another. Trust me, it's not worth spending time talking about. Very boring."

"So what *is* worth spending time talking about? All I really see on the forms you submitted, at least that stands out to me, is the word 'anger.'"

Richard's hands slid to the ends of the chair arms and gripped tightly.

"Yeah. As a kid, even a teenager, something would happen, or someone would do something annoying. Like anyone else, I'd be mad, think it through, and then let it go. Most of the time, I would forget about it."

"And now?" Justin asked.

"Now I can't let anything go. I looked it up on Google. It's called rumination. Thinking about something over and over and over. It can be a little thing like someone not holding the door open for me. Or rolling their shopping cart down the wrong side of the supermarket aisle. I can't let it go. I end up hating that person, and I'll think about it all day, even sometimes at night when I'm trying to fall asleep. I picture their face, and anger takes over." He stopped talking as his knuckles went pale from squeezing the chair arms. "You should've seen me on the way here. Walking down Park Avenue, I despised everyone I saw. Everyone. And I have no idea why."

Justin opened his journal. *Anger rumination.*

"Here's a question. Did you wake up feeling anger or irritation this morning?"

"I kind of have it all the time. But it's usually at a lower level when I first wake up."

"Did something happen at work? On the street? Can you re-member when your button got pressed, so to speak?"

"Not really. But even when my anger doesn't get stoked by something, it just, well, simmers. There are days I *don't* feel as bad as I do today. It'll be. . . how do I put it? It'll only be a slight hostility toward humanity." He brushed away strands of the thin brown hair falling over his sky blue eyes. "Then there are days like today when I can't help but hate everyone I see, and it feels like it's eating me up inside. Like it burns in the pit of my stomach and spreads from there until my whole body feels sick."

"Well, since you're feeling this anger so intensely today, I'm glad you're here. It might make it easier for us to find the root cause or causes of how you're feeling. You said you didn't wake up with this *extreme* anger and hatred, right? So I'm wondering what might have set things off. I don't care how small you think it might be. It could be even less than the shopping cart scenario or door-holding situation. Maybe someone looked at you in a way you didn't like. . . perhaps somewhat disrespectfully."

Richard looked up at the ceiling and then closed his eyes. Knit-ting his brow, he turned his head toward the window and opened his eyes again.

"I got nothing," he said. "I was okay leaving the house and at work. Then, it started on my walk here. Seeing all those people. The mass of heads and bodies, like zombies searching for a source of food." He subtly shook his head and looked at Justin.

"I'm sure it sounds ridiculous," he said, "but when I look at them, I can see that no one gives a shit about each other. If one of them had a heart attack and fell on the sidewalk, everyone would just walk over them. Why? Because no matter what, they still need to reach their food source."

Justin continued to scribble in his journal. *Misanthropy caused by: anxiety? depression? antisocial personality disorder?*

"You're writing a lot," Richard said.

"I apologize. If it bothers you, I can stop. I like to have notes to go back to when and if the time comes. It's your call whether or not to continue taking them."

Richard wiped his eyes with his palms. "No, it's fine." He started tapping his foot on the rug beneath him. "As long as it helps, I'm all for it," he added.

Justin finished writing and clicked his pen closed. "First of all, Richard, nothing sounds 'ridiculous' in this office. If you think about it and feel it, then it's important. Please, don't worry about what *I* think about your feelings. Second, it sounds to me like the energy of Manhattan is a lot for you. This is New York City. There's noise, commotion, and, most of all, people. Some thrive on it; others don't. Can I ask how long you've lived here?"

"My whole life," he answered.

"You said you could handle your anger as a child, even as a teenager. You could let go of experiences that initially made you angry or frustrated. And now you're saying you can't. Do you have any idea when this struggle to let things go started?"

Straight away, Richard shook his head. "No," he said. "I don't."

He's lying, Justin thought. He saw it in the shift of the man's expression, heard it in the tremor of his voice. *Something to delve into when he feels more comfortable.*

"Okay, well, we'll get more into that at another time. I would like to know if you've ever acted on your feelings — say, by yelling, pushing someone... or even hurting them."

"No," Richard said vehemently.

"Have you ever *wanted* to hurt someone or fantasized about it?"

A few seconds went by before Richard shook his head.

"No, never."

"Not even fantasized about it?"

An angry expression overtook his face. He shook his head without making a sound.

Another lie.

Justin waited.

"I told you, Doctor Wright. It's hurting *me.* No one else. I can feel it in my gut, eating me up inside. And *that's* what I need to stop. It will kill me before I have a chance to live."

"Okay, Richard. I hear you. Together we'll make sure that doesn't happen."

"Yeah," he muttered under his breath. "I'm sure you've said those words before."

Justin leaned forward. "Pardon? I didn't hear you."

"Nothing."

"No, Richard. I need you to repeat what you said."

Richard took in a deep breath and exhaled hard through his lips.

"I said, 'I'm sure you've said those words before.' You know, that you won't let anything happen. Then it happened. Because you can't control everything people think... or do. You can try, but you can't."

A wave of nausea crashed into Justin's gut, Richard's words echoing his own self-blame for not protecting Dylan, allowing something to happen to his son that he couldn't control. *Not now,* he said to himself. *Not now.*

The images of Dylan and swell of sadness inside made Justin want to reach over and place his hand on the young man's shoulder. He was clearly in pain and had lived through one, if not several, experiences that led him to his office today. Richard seemed to hate not only people but also life — and possibly himself.

"You're right, Richard. I can't control what people think or do. I can only try to help them the best I can. And the same goes for you. We can work together to help you through this, but I can't control your thoughts or actions. I can only try to help you see things differently so you can live a life you deserve, not one you despise."

Richard hung his head as though ashamed of his own words. But by his tone, Justin knew he had meant every syllable. *I'm sure you've said that before.* The sentence stuck like a leech inside the walls of Justin's skull. It took him a few seconds longer than he wanted to shake it free, but he knew it would be back.

"What about your girlfriend?" Justin asked, changing the subject. "What's her name?"

"We don't need to talk names yet. Let's make sure this is going to work between us before getting into real personal detail."

Justin leaned back and rubbed the clicker of his pen along his bottom lip. "I apologize," he said. "You tell me about your anger and hatred toward humanity, yet your *girlfriend's name* is a personal detail? I didn't realize that."

"Well, now you do," Richard countered.

The tension in the room was as thick as the humidity outside, and Justin had to lighten it — quickly.

"Got it," he replied. "Do you ever experience animosity or loathing toward her?"

"No."

"Why not, do you think?"

"She's never done anything to make me angry. And if she does, well, I guess we talk about it."

"And the people on the street you passed today, what did they do to make you angry?"

"Nothing."

"So why do you... as you put it... 'hate' them?"

Richard glanced around the room like the answer would drip down one of the generic watercolors hanging on the walls. His gaze finally came to rest on Justin's eyes.

"Like I said before, I guess it's because they don't care."

"Care about what?"

Richard let go of the chair arms and leaned against one, folding his legs. Then he unfolded them. Although this uncomfortable fidgeting typically meant he and his patient were getting close to something important, Justin had to make sure not to push things too far, especially during an initial session.

He replaced his expression of concern with one of compassion before repeating his question. "What is it these strangers don't care about, Richard?"

"About me and everyone around them, I guess."

"Are you saying everyone should care about you and who you are?"

"Not everyone," he answered, almost whispering, like an embarrassed five-year-old on the verge of tears.

"Do you care about everyone around *you*?"

Richard folded his legs again, and he picked at the rubber sole of his sneaker.

"Do you?"

"All I know is if I was hit by a car on Madison Avenue, people would walk right over me, like the guy I talked about before who had the heart attack. In this city, I'd be lucky if anyone even called 9-1-1."

Justin moved forward in his chair.

"Do you think *I* care about you and who you are?" Justin asked.

Richard looked him directly in the eyes, his expression blank, his lips pursed.

"Not really," he replied. "Well... not yet. But I have a feeling you will pretty soon."

CHAPTER 3

N o matter how hard she tried to hold it down, the lump in Mandy's throat rose until it became difficult to speak.

Bach's Brandenburg Concerto no. 3 in G major floated from room to room, playing softly through the home sound system Dylan had installed for them. The classical music, and the memory of who made it possible to enjoy the concerto, was what first created the tightness in her throat. Now, sitting on the sofa with Michael, each of them with one arm stretched across the edge of its backrest and clasping fingers, the swelling in her throat was close to painful.

The position was the same as she and Dylan sat on the night of the visit that ended with him and Justin fighting about everything from Kyle's medication to Dylan's state of mind. Her memories, along with the sad expression on Michael's face as he stared out the back wall of windows, raised a lump in her throat that made it seem impossible to swallow without her son noticing.

She let go of his fingers and ran her nails gently through the hair on the back of his head. So soft, almost silky to the touch, just as she remembered from his childhood. Michael didn't move.

He gazed out into the yard, where yellow hydrangea flowers bent under their own weight until they lay across the windowsill.

"We're going to have to get those trimmed," she said. "They'll start crawling inside the house and take over the dining room table." She hoped a little humor would break the silence and semi-somber mood.

It didn't.

"Trim what?" asked Michael.

"Those hydrangeas. See how they're getting onto the windowsill?"

"Oh, yeah," he said, his voice sounding as melancholy as the concerto's cellos. "I didn't know what they were called."

"We planted them the summer before you..." She caught herself. "Almost eight years ago. They've really grown."

Michael let go a quick puff of air from between his lips. "Mom, don't worry. You're allowed to talk about it. Why don't I say it for you? 'We planted them the summer before you were taken.'" He shook his head as though she'd made a mistake she could never seem to learn from. She silently cursed herself, knowing his head shaking was well-deserved. Why did she keep avoiding the topic she constantly longed for him to talk about? She'd ask Justin for the answer if he hadn't done the same thing himself so often.

She stopped stroking his hair and slid her arm across the backrest to her side.

"I'm sorry, Michael. But please, give me a little break here. Sometimes I don't know what to say or if anything even should be said. I don't want to bring up bad memories. I don't want to hurt you. I don't want to make you feel bad in *any* way. So forgive

24

me. I'm not an expert at how to handle this... how to act when my son returns after being gone for seven years."

The lump expanded, making her voice weaker.

"It's okay, Mom. Just say what you want to say. I won't hold it against you. Lauren explained how all of this stuff is uncharted... uncharted... shit, what's the word?"

"Territory?" Mandy offered.

"Yeah, it's new for all of us. It's like a map with a beginning point and an end point but no directions in between. She said we have to find our way the best we can, together, to get to the destination."

Mandy smiled as relief swept through her. He had finally given some detail about what he and Lauren had talked about. Thank God Lauren had brought up that she and Justin would work *with* Michael to bring some normalcy back into their lives.

"And what is the destination?" she asked. "Did Lauren say?"

Michael looked at her, running his own fingers through his hair. His eyes appeared a darker brown than when she'd gazed into them at the hospital in Pennsylvania the day of his return. They had more depth, more life, a look of hope — all helping to release more of her tension, including the lump straining in her throat.

"Happiness," Michael said. "To be able to enjoy life. What happened to me will always affect me. But she said I'll learn to process it in a way that makes me stronger. Physically and emotionally. She always says, 'It's all about joy — not just being able to talk about what is and how it *should* feel, but being able to experience it from the inside out.' It takes me time to make sense of things she says, but her words just *feel* right. I don't know; maybe it's *how* she says them."

Mandy's entire body took a breath. This was the progress she'd been waiting for, the opening up she'd fantasized about for so long. She wondered if Michael would ever talk with her and Justin about those seven years away from them — what he went through, how he felt, what the days and nights were like for him. When she was honest with herself, she wasn't sure she wanted to know. How would she handle it? What would she say? Would her reaction only make things worse?

Even *thinking* about what he might have lived through already tore her heart to shreds. How was she going to manage *listening* to the horror from Michael's lips? She dreaded the day he'd tell them, but she also longed for it, knowing that letting him share those truths would help him in ways no touch or kiss on the forehead ever could.

"As long as you're talking with her and she helps you feel better," Mandy replied. "Just know that your dad and I love you more than you could ever imagine, and we're here for you no matter what. If you need to talk, cry, or scream at two in the morning, just bang on our door. I don't want you ever to feel alone. It's the three of us now, and no one and nothing will change that."

The moment she placed her hand on his, Justin walked in the front door. They turned to him as he threw his keys on the console table. He missed the bowl by about five inches and, cursing under his breath, walked into the living room.

In hopes of relieving the mood revealed by his language and the frown on his face, Mandy tried a little humor.

"Bad day, I presume?" she asked, smiling at Michael.

Justin plopped down on the accent chair and glanced at both of them.

"Are you laughing at me?" he asked. Mandy was happy he played along, even though the lines his frown had carved around his mouth and eyes lingered, easy to see from across the room.

"Obviously," Michael replied. "You don't usually. . ."

"Scowl?" Mandy suggested.

As she laughed with their son, she glanced at Justin, hoping he was doing the same.

He was.

"Yeah, yeah. Funny. Bad day. I think my new patient is rubbing off on me." He leaned back in the chair.

"What's wrong with her. . . or him?" Michael asked.

Justin pinched the bridge of his nose, closing his eyes. Mandy predicted that he'd force a slight smile, and again, he didn't disappoint. "Nothing's 'wrong' with my patients," he said. "They just have problems that need addressing."

She laughed again. "Well, what does this patient need addressed?"

"He suffers from anger rumination. In professional terms, it's a cognitive-emotional process, a tendency to dwell on frustrating circumstances and recall past anger experiences. In layman's terms, you know, like for the two of you. . ." *Touché!* ". . . it translates into this particular person being constantly mad at the people and world around him because of an inability to let anything go, no matter how unimportant or insignificant it may be."

"Well. . ." Mandy remarked. "From the look on your face when you walked in the door and the very serious tone in your voice, I'd say you have a bit of anger rumination going on right now."

"I'm about to," Justin scoffed.

He gave Mandy a subtle wink and turned to Michael.

"Hey, son," he started. "Before we eat dinner, there are a few things we wanted to talk with you about."

"Shoot," Michael said, crossing his arms and then his ankles.

"Well, first, I hope you know that your mom and I love you more than —"

"We just went through that before you got home," Michael interrupted. "You're here for me twenty-four-seven no matter what I need. Got it."

Mandy saw a twinge of both pain and embarrassment cross Justin's face. "Michael, please, come on now," she said. "There's no need to be so curt."

"Sorry," Michael conceded. "Whattaya got? What did you want to talk about?"

Justin let out a sigh. "First let's talk about your visit with Anthony."

"I told you, he's an asshole. I didn't —"

"Language, please," Justin stated sharply. "I know you said you didn't enjoy the visit. That wasn't what I wanted to talk about. It's that Lauren said you told her meeting Anthony was fine with us, and we gave you permission. You told her your mother was willing to drive you into Westchester. Meanwhile, you never even mentioned him to either of us. Why is that?"

"Privacy," Michael said without hesitation. "I'm here all the time. You guys see and hear everything I do. I just wanted to get away for a little while, knowing there weren't eyes watching my every move."

Justin nodded. "Okay, I get that. I do. But then Lauren said she left me a voicemail. When I checked my phone, there was no sign that she had called or left a message. I find that strange."

Michael uncrossed his arms and laid his hands on his lap. He then lowered his head and studied the looms of the rug.

"Michael? Did you hear me?"

There was no sign he had.

"Michael, please. Just answer me. I — we need to know what happened to that message. If you have any idea, tell us."

Michael raised his head. He glanced at Mandy and looked at Justin.

"I erased it." His voice was barely audible.

Mandy's upper body tensed as she tried to read Michael's expression. He didn't appear ashamed or embarrassed, not sad or angry. There was only pure indifference, no indication that he understood what he did was wrong. Her tension spread throughout her entire body.

"Why?" asked Justin.

"I already told you. I wanted some privacy. Something of my own that the two of you didn't know about. I'm not being mean, but sometimes I feel like I'm under a microscope, and I... I don't know. I just need some breathing room."

Justin leaned back in the chair. Mandy held her breath, the all too recent memory of his and Dylan's fight pushing its way into her thoughts. She would not let it happen with Michael, too. Still, she'd agreed with Justin that they needed to have this conversation. She decided she would give him some leeway — until she wouldn't.

"Okay, I get that, too, Michael. And we apologize. We're both doing the best we can. *However,* my phone is as private as your phone. It has messages and texts from clients and colleagues that are extremely confidential. I can't have anyone, *anyone,* reading them."

"I'm sorry," Michael said.

Mandy wanted to grab his hand and kiss it. Tell him everything was okay, and she knew he had learned his lesson. But she had to let Justin get the point across without either of them being too lenient. There were rules for Michael to follow in their home, and if he said he wanted privacy, he had to respect theirs too.

"Apology accepted." Justin took a breath. "Okay, now there's something a little more complicated I need to bring up." He and Mandy waited in vain for a response from Michael. "Well, Frank Devlin, who you know as Nathan, implied that you had something to do with Berny Malone's death."

Michael looked between them. "Berny who?"

"My friend Berny, the head of psychiatry at Bellevue who accidentally fell — or so we think — off the terrace of his sixtieth-floor apartment the other night."

"Why would I have anything to do with *that*? I didn't even know the guy. And what night are you talking about?"

Mandy glanced at Justin and gave a tiny nod.

She told Michael, "It was the night you said that Lauren told you going for walks is good for you. You said you were going into town and having some dinner, but you didn't get home until almost midnight."

"See what I mean? You're keeping track of every move I make!" Beads of sweat dotted his forehead as he fidgeted on the sofa. "I thought I was done with that. I thought I was free."

Michael's veiled accusation made Mandy flinch, and it took all the strength she had to hold back the flood of tears.

"Michael, baby. Please don't say that. You're free to come and go as you please. It's just that I heard the front door open and looked at the clock. That's not keeping tabs on you; that's just wanting to know the time."

"Where did you eat?" Justin asked. Michael's eyes narrowed, and Mandy winced. She was trying to calm their son down, and Justin's investigatory questions were only making him more uncomfortable.

"Poppy's," he snapped. "I went to Poppy's and had a burger and fries. Wanna go ask them to monitor the son you love so much?"

"Watch your tone, Michael."

"Justin, please!" Mandy begged, holding back tears.

Michael picked at his cuticles. "You know, you told me not to believe anything Nathan said. Now you're telling me *you* believed him when he said I had something to do with this guy falling off a terrace. Which is it? Should we believe him or not?"

"Honey," Mandy said, lightly touching his arm. "We asked you not to believe his lies about Kyle's involvement in your kidnapping or Dylan's death. Since we *knew* he wasn't involved in any way, we were adamant about not even considering what Nathan had to say. The Berny Malone thing is different because —"

"Because why?" Michael asked as he stood, sliding his hands into his pants pockets. "Do you think I had something to do with Kyle killing himself, too? Do you think the last seven years turned me into the Crazy Killer of Rye?"

Justin got up and went after Michael. He caught up with him at the foot of the staircase, where his son stood holding onto the round glass finial of the bottom post.

"Like I told Lauren," — Michael's voice rose and filled with anger — "I'm not a hundred percent sure of anything right now. But the one thing I am sure of is that I'm not a murderer!"

Justin called his name as he ran up the stairs. They heard his door slam. Then silence.

The lump in Mandy's throat finally passed its breaking point, and tears ran down her cheeks like a fountain had been turned on.

"I don't... I can't... I..." She tried speaking through her tears, but her thoughts weren't clear enough to finish a sentence.

Justin sat beside her and stroked the back of her head.

"I'm texting Lauren right now," he said. "We need to meet with her as soon as possible."

CHAPTER 4

The Day Room was about half full. A few patients stared vacantly at the television; others sat at small round tables biting on puzzle pieces, searching for the one spot in which that lonely piece might fit. Others, like the woman Nathan watched, sat silent, gazing out the giant windows at a world that might have been their oyster if they hadn't been who they were.

Looking at the empty seat next to Jade, he knew it was time to make his move. He'd seen her walking around, usually by herself. Sometimes she'd be mumbling; other times, she was silent, staring straight ahead as though no one else existed or mattered. And at other times, she'd seemed almost normal. She even returned his "hi" a few times, offering a nod or a fake smile. But she'd never given him enough reaction to determine where he stood with her. What's her story... and why would Justin Wright leave his hoity-toity office to visit her?

He slid his slippered feet in her direction until he stood in front of the chair next to hers.

"May I sit?" he asked, holding the back.

Jade glanced up at him, then returned her gaze out the window.

"Whatever," she replied.

Nathan sat down. "That's quite an invitation."

Her lack of response, positive or negative, told him sarcasm would not work.

"I'm Nathan," he said.

"You sure?"

Hmmm, maybe she does *like sarcasm.*

"Good one." He laughed. "Yeah, I'm sure. You're Jade, right?"

"You know who I am. Everyone here knows everything."

"Angry much?"

Jade slowly turned her head and looked directly into his eyes.

"As angry as you, Nathan."

Now she waited for his response. When he didn't give her one, she looked back out the window.

"I hear you killed your husband's brother," he said as casually as he would about the weather.

"I hear you killed Justin Wright's son," she retorted.

He nodded, then asked, "You don't talk to anyone. How would *you* know why I'm here?"

Jade let out a sigh. "I'll tell you how, Nathan. I was in the downstairs lobby one day and met this really nice guy. His name was Kyle. He was here to visit Frank Devlin... well, actually, he was here to visit his boyfriend, Matthew. Do any of those names ring a bell in that head of yours... or theirs... or whoever?"

Nathan chuckled. "You're a real smartass, aren't you?" No response. "I like that. And yes, I know Frank *and* Matthew. They pretty much don't exist anymore. They are two weak losers who are powerless now because, as *you* probably understand better than anyone, only the strong survive."

Jade crossed her arms and continued gazing out the window.

"Yeah," Nathan said, annoyed by the silence. "Only the strong survive. Unlike your friend, Kyle."

Jade closed her eyes, then slowly opened them. She turned to look at Nathan and studied his face before speaking.

"What are you talking about? Did something happen to Kyle?"

Nathan smiled. "Oh, wow. I guess everyone here *doesn't* know everything, huh?" he asked, wanting to keep her in suspense.

"Tell me," she said, her voice getting angry.

"Why do you care?" he asked, her uneasy look delighting him from deep inside.

Jade turned her head, her body almost squirming as she stared into his eyes.

"Because I do, you asshole. Now tell me what happened to Kyle, or I'll make your life a living hell."

Nathan threw his head back and laughed.

"Oh, will you?" he asked. "And how would you do that?"

"How about I tell the nurses… or maybe even security, that you raped me. They'll throw you in solitary before you have a chance to say the word 'liar'. I'm a pretty good actress," she leaned forward in her chair and forced tears from her eyes. "I can start right now if you'd like."

Fuck. She's good. Almost as good as me.

"He's dead." Nathan blurted.

"What do you mean?"

Nathan loved being the bearer of bad news.

"Dead. As in D-E-A-D." He spelled it out, hoping it would add a bit more devastation.

"What happened... How... When...?"

"A few days ago, I think. I heard he took one too many of his meds. A real pill popper, that one."

Jade grabbed her tightly wrapped ponytail and tugged on it. In a matter of seconds, her expression turned from sadness to anger. Perhaps they were more alike than he originally thought.

"It's your fault!" she said, almost shouting. A nurse glanced their way, and in a softer tone, Jade repeated, "Your fault."

"What are you saying? How could it be my fault?" Nathan crossed his legs and set his elbow on his knee. Though the posture was mocking, it wasn't an act; he was truly interested, about to learn some earth-shattering news.

"When Kyle came to see you — I mean Matthew — he was all excited. He loved Matthew and couldn't wait to talk to him. But when we were both in the Day Room, and I saw him talking to you, he looked upset. Devastated. He was crying as he walked to the elevator." She scraped her fingers through her ponytail. "What did you say to him?"

"That's for me to know and you to find out," he joked.

"What are you, a four-year-old? We're talking about someone's life here. A nice, sweet guy whose life you probably destroyed."

Nathan held his hand up like a crossing guard stopping cars. "Hold up, missy. The killer of an innocent man is telling *me* that *I* destroyed a life? Are you *kidding* me with this?"

"Fuck you," she whispered.

"No, fuck you, Pot. I'm the kettle you're calling black, and I don't like it."

Jade leaned over in her chair until her face was only inches from his.

"I don't give a shit *what* you like or don't like. I'm not here to please *you*. Now get away from me before I get a security guard to *take* you away."

Nathan fell back in his chair to put some distance between the two of them. She was beautiful, yet tough. He liked that. She was strong, yet he sensed a hint of vulnerability, and *that* was the piece of her he wanted to get to know better. But first, he'd have to make nice.

"I'm sorry," he said. "I apologize. I felt bad when I first heard about Kyle," he lied. "But if I took responsibility for it, the guilt would haunt me for the rest of my life." He looked to the tile floor and scooted his slippered feet back and forth across it. "And I already feel guilty enough about what I did to Dylan Wright."

Jade rolled her eyes and sighed. "Whatever," he thought she said, but her voice was so low he hardly heard her.

They sat silently for a few minutes before Nathan raised the subject he'd been waiting to talk about, something he hoped would soften her up a bit.

"Just an FYI, I used to talk to your mother all the time." He kept his eyes staring out the window, not wanting to come across as too forward while he raised this delicate matter.

"Great," she replied.

"She was a decent lady. Always kept me entertained."

"Really? How did she do that?"

"Told me lots of stories."

From the corner of his eye, he saw Jade shaking her head as she laughed. "Lots of stories, huh? How many?"

Nathan slapped his thigh, chuckling. "Okay, you got me. She only told me one story."

"Do I ask which story it was, or would you like me to guess?"

"You can guess if you'd like," he responded as he dared a glance at her face. *Damn it!* Despite her laughter, she didn't appear to be softening yet.

"Let me think, was there any mention of the Brady Bunch?"

Nathan laughed again. "Ha. Yeah. That would be the one."

"Did she give you the details?"

"Uh, yeah."

"Did she tell you how I walked in and saw my father's head hanging by a shred of skin?"

"Yeah."

Jade looked around the room. "Jesus. And you wonder why I'm in here."

Nathan put his hand on the back of her chair.

"I don't wonder," he said softly. He'd heard that sometimes gentleness was all it took to break through someone's shell. Though he'd never tried it before, now might be the time. "When you go through something like that, it affects you. I can't imagine what it must've been —"

"And what did *you* go through?" She cut him off. "What happened to you that landed you in this nuthouse? And most likely prison in five or six months? Huh? What happened to *you*?"

Fire kindled inside the pit of Nathan's stomach. A bead of sweat dripped down his back, tickling as it made its way to the elastic band of his briefs. *She's smart,* he thought, *trying to piss me off.* He sat straight and attempted to shake off the anger that buzzed through his entire body like an electric current.

"Your mother," he said. "Same story over and over again. She never shut up. Well, until... until they found her hanging in her room."

Now we'll see who can piss whom off the most.

There was no change in her demeanor or her expression. The rhythm of her breathing didn't even change. *She's good.*

"So, here's a question for you, *Jade*. Do you think she did it to herself or someone did it to her?"

The shock on Jade's face showed he'd found the g-spot of her vulnerability. She sat up straighter in her chair and now turned her entire body toward him.

"What are you saying?"

"I'm just saying that around here, you never know. People think we're crazy, so if they find someone hanging from a bathroom door, they're going to assume it's a suicide."

"Are you saying she might have been murdered? Why would someone murder my mother?"

Nathan stood up, wiped his palms on his tee shirt as if to iron out the wrinkles, and walked behind her chair. He bent down and whispered in her ear.

"Like I said, in this place, you never know. Could've been something as insignificant as a roll of toilet paper."

He left her sitting there, her face blank as she processed it — the smile never leaving his own face as he walked through the maze of corridors all the way back to his room.

CHAPTER 5

J ustin and Mandy sat next to one another on the velour-cushioned couch. Mandy had one of the three mustard-colored cushions on her lap and picked at the fringes projecting out from the shredding seam.

"Like mother, like son," Lauren said with a smile, sitting in the chair across from them.

"What do you mean, Dr. Murphy?" Mandy clasped her hands and lay them on top of the pillow.

"Please call me Lauren. I meant that Michael also pulls at those little tendrils coming out of the pillow. Which reminds me, I think it's time to get some new ones, this time without such easy-to-pluck threading."

Justin wasn't particularly interested in the therapist's future decor selection. Listening to her speak, he started to wonder if Van Sessler had recommended the best psychiatrist for his son.

"Lauren, we're here to talk about Michael, not your pillows. Now I —"

"Justin!" Mandy interrupted. "That was rude. Why would you say that? Would *you* ever talk like that to a patient?"

"Lauren isn't a patient. She's our son's therapist who has been in session with him more than —"

"Please, please," Lauren intervened. "No worries. I understand. I've been there myself. Not in your exact position, but in a place where I've lost my patience and just want answers." She looked directly at Justin. "Talk to me. I know most of your concerns, but I want to hear anything else you and Mandy would like to know — things that won't violate therapist-patient confidentiality, of course, nothing Michael might have asked me not to share."

All morning, Justin had thought about how to best approach the subject of Kyle and Berny without putting the thought in her head that Michael might be involved. Then again, she might already suspect something and be waiting for the right time to tell them. He was all too familiar with the limits of confidentiality when it came to harm — to the patient's self or to others. She'd talk to Michael, gather enough evidence to inform the police, and then turn him in...

It almost made his head spin to realize where his mind had wandered. Maybe the run-in with Devlin had created more internal conflict than he'd first thought. *Shit. I'm losing my edge.*

He said, "We're a little concerned that Michael may have been involved with something that might cause legal issues down the line. We don't know what he tells you, and we don't ask, but we'd like to be prepared."

There, I said it.

He had tried coming up with a more subtle way of broaching the subject, but his mind drew nothing but blanks. Now his anxiety was on the rise as he feared his impatience had gotten the better of him and he should have completely avoided the word 'legal.'

He leaned into the back of the couch, then took Mandy's hand from the pillow and clutched it.

Lauren crossed her legs, looking between them both. For a moment, Justin saw the psychiatrist in her face as she prepared herself — measuring her statement, ensuring she wouldn't say too much... or too little.

"Okay, I'm assuming your concern involves your family friends Kyle and Doctor Malone," Lauren said. "Let me just say I know this information because Michael brought it up, and we discussed it." She paused and offered the beginning of a smile. "In my professional opinion, your son did not hurt anyone."

"Can you say that with complete and absolute certainty?" Justin asked.

"Would you say that on the witness stand?" Mandy added.

Lauren's calm expression hardened. "What makes you think there will be a witness stand? And if there was, who would accuse Michael of anything? Would it be you, the police, Kyle's family? All I can tell you is, as of right now, the accusation would not be coming from me."

"Lauren," Justin said, "we're not accusing Michael of anything. For God's sake, he's our son! The *last* thing we want to think is that he... It's just that he rarely speaks, never shows emotion, and leaves the house without telling us where he's going or when he's coming back. When I looked at his phone, everything had been deleted. His calls, his texts, everything. I really don't know —"

"Wait," Lauren stopped him in his tracks. "Are you saying you've been snooping around on Michael's phone?"

You mean the way he was snooping around on my phone? "Don't go there," he almost said aloud.

"Well, I just wanted to see if his geo-tracker was on, and if maybe there was a way I could see where he was... and when. Or even just find out who he might be talking to. Someone who might be up to no good. But I didn't come up with anything."

Lauren placed her index finger over her mouth. Again, Justin recognized the kind of processing he did in his own profession as she attempted to find the right words.

"Justin, by looking at his phone, you *are,* in essence, accusing him. Michael has been opening up more and more during each of our sessions. As you know, people who go through trauma develop their own coping mechanisms, children as well as adults." She took a deep breath. "Now, I'm not trying to be insensitive here or accusatory. However, with what you've been through with Devlin and the way *he* coped with *his* childhood traumas, your thinking may be leaning in a direction that I don't think is appropriate when it comes to Michael."

Justin nodded and felt Mandy squeeze his hand.

"I know you're both tired of hearing me say, 'give it time,' but honestly, it's the only way through this. To put it bluntly, Michael was held captive for seven years. Two to three months of therapy will not turn him around and bring things back to exactly where they were before those seven years. In fact, they never *will* be where they were. Everything is different, and *our* job is to help Michael live the best life possible in a world that has changed for him, both inside and out."

"What about this Anthony kid? Can you tell us anything about that?"

"I can tell you that Anthony was held captive by Alfred Dingle for two years. Michael was held for seven. I'm not saying that two years don't create their own trauma. In my work, I've seen how two *days* can have a significant effect on one's psyche. But Michael went through a lot more for a longer period of time. That means there's more... *much* more to process. Plus, Anthony is a different person, which means he handles things in other ways than Michael, or anyone else for that matter. He sorts them out in his own way. His psychological makeup is his own. This means we can't expect the same outcome for two distinct individuals." She looked at Justin and leaned forward. "I feel like I'm preaching to the choir. You know all these things, Justin. The problem, in this case, is your relationship with the patient. When it's *this* personal, logic, expertise, and past client experience can often be overlooked or temporarily lost."

Justin nodded and let go of Mandy's hand, leaning his elbows on his knees.

"Yes, I- we get that. I guess we're wondering why he never brought Anthony up before. It's like this kid came out of the blue."

"Independence. Privacy. Autonomy. Michael hasn't been able to enjoy these things for seven years. Anything he's allowed to have for himself, without anyone else knowing about it, is, well, a gift of sorts. Anthony was his secret, his gift. He came out of the blue when Michael decided to share his gift."

Again, Justin nodded. "I hear you," he mumbled. "I can't say I completely agree, but I hear you."

Lauren didn't move. She looked at Mandy, who was trying to wipe the tears from her face before they reached her chin.

"The other night — " Mandy began before grabbing a tissue off the side table. She used it to dab her cheeks and wipe her nose.

"The other night, we had such a great talk with Michael. He was telling us how much you were helping him and some things you talked about. And then, it was just like his personality changed. He got angry and defensive. He went on a rant and then ran up the stairs and slammed the door. I felt like we went back to square one."

Lauren pursed her lips. "Did something happen in between your talk and his 'rant,' as you call it?"

Justin cleared his throat. "Well, we started to ask him about Berny. Then Devlin came up in the conversation and —"

"I think I get the picture," Lauren said. "Think about the questions he was being asked and how they might have affected him. If you were a scared teenager faced with a confrontational situation, do you think you might have run away? Up the stairs? Out the door? To anywhere the conflict wasn't taking place?"

Justin and Mandy nodded in unison.

"You're right," Justin said, guilt softening the tone of his voice.

Mandy said, "I have to ask something that's been on my mind for quite a while." She inhaled deeply, hesitated for a few seconds, then let out a breath. "I'll just come right out and ask it... do you think Michael might have alters?"

Lauren looked up at the ceiling and pursed her lips. Justin watched her gather her thoughts. "There are facets of his personality that were developing when he was taken. And they're still developing today. My goal is to give him time to integrate these aspects of his natural makeup and individuality so he can feel comfortable inside his mind and body. It's up to *us* to give him the freedom, support, and help to do that now since he hasn't had the chance to do it for seven years." She sat back in her chair. "That's a long way of saying 'no, I don't think Michael has alters.' I think some of his development might have been delayed, and his moods, tone and confusion about who he is at times is proof of that delay."

A few seconds of silence and stillness passed before Mandy threw her tissues into the wastebasket beside her and crossed her arms. The look on her face had switched from mother to attorney. Justin's stomach twisted; he knew what was coming.

"I believe with all my heart that Michael is innocent of any wrongdoing. And since you said that *right now* you wouldn't accuse Michael of anything, I believe you feel the same way." Justin heard Mandy's breath intensify with every word she spoke. "But you never really answered my original question, Lauren," Mandy said.

"What question is that?"

"If you were on the witness stand and asked if Michael had anything to do with Kyle or Berny Malone's death, would you say you are one hundred percent sure Michael was not involved and did not harm a soul?"

Lauren shuffled in her chair and clasped her hands. She glanced at Justin and then at Mandy.

"Today, sitting on *this* witness stand, I'd say I was one hundred percent sure." She looked at her hands, then again at Justin and Mandy. "However, Michael and I have quite a few sessions to go, so I can't promise that will always be the case."

CHAPTER 6

J en knocked on the door and turned to Keith. His expression told her he knew what she was thinking, most likely because he felt the same way.

"When was the last time we were here?" she asked.

"Almost a year ago," Keith answered. "Too long."

Jen nodded in agreement as the heavy wooden door opened.

A handsome young man stood before them. He wore a black V-neck T-shirt with an odd logo on it — for a rock band, she presumed, one she'd never heard of. His shorts were salmon-colored, a shade whose popularity she could never understand. It made her think of rotting flesh, and she forbade Keith from ever buying clothing of that color. The young man's blue Sperry boat sneakers looked worn, their frayed fabric hanging over muddy soles. It appeared as though he'd bought them many years ago and hadn't found the time or money to purchase a new pair.

He blew the thin wisps of hair off his forehead and smiled. Jen looked into his light brown eyes and forced a smile in return.

"Hi," she said. "We're Kyle's parents. You must be Rick."

"Oh my God," he said. "Yes, I'm Rick. Please, come in."

As they walked down the hallway toward the living room, Jen grabbed Keith's arm. *This is where he lived,* she thought. *And this is where he died.* She felt faint.

He took her hand and led her the rest of the way. All the windows were open, allowing a light cross breeze to cool them off. The apartment held the same shabby furnishings she remembered, with rugs just as dingy. She saw half-packed moving boxes scattered throughout the living room, dining room, and hallway up the three stairs leading to the bedrooms.

"Are you moving out?" she asked, tightening her grip around Keith's arm.

"Yeah," Rick said. "I'm not really comfortable living here with everything that happened." He looked at the floor and scooted his foot along a dusty plank, plainly embarrassed. "I mean, I just think it's time for a new place. I've already moved a lot of stuff into my girlfriend Andrea's place uptown. I'll stay there for now, and then, who knows?"

Leaning on Ken's support, she moved toward the sofa so she could sit. "I'm sorry," she said. "I'm just feeling a little dizzy."

"Not a problem," Rick replied. "Can I get you some water or something? I think I have a bottle of — "

"No, no. Please, don't bother. I'll be okay in a minute." Jen looked around and took a deep breath, hoping to smell the scent of Kyle. Maybe his hair, his skin, something that told her he once lived a real life in this place. She didn't smell a thing other than cardboard boxes and the exhaust from a truck that had just sped by the brownstone.

"So," Keith said. "The landlord is letting you out of the lease?"

"Actually, the lease was in Kyle's name. The landlord let me stay here month-to-month. He said my decision to leave was perfect timing because he has two people who can move in next month. He's going to repaint and fix the place up a little after I leave. Anyway, he was nice enough to let me stay this long, and he's pretty psyched about the new tenants."

"Good," Keith said. "That's good."

Jen heard the vacant tone in his voice and watched the sadness creep into his face. It was time to get past her lightheadedness and take the lead.

"We're here to pick up the rest of Kyle's things. You were kind enough to pack up and deliver most of them, but you said there were some personal items you weren't sure what to do with. We're here to bring them home with us."

"Yeah, I didn't want to take a chance sending them in the mail. These days you never know," Rick said, walking toward the stairs leading to the bedrooms.

"Before we take them," Keith said, "I want to apologize for how we haven't spoken to you before today. We know you're the one who found Kyle, and it must have been... well, just awful. I'm so sorry you had to go through that."

Rick kept his eyes glued to the floor. "No need to apologize. Yeah, it was rough. But not as rough as it must be on you. I wish I knew he was feeling so bad about things." Rick paused and finally looked at the both of them. "He pretty much kept to himself. Didn't talk much. Maybe I should've known something was up. Maybe I could have — "

"Don't," Keith said. "If anyone should have known, it should've been us." He slid his hands into his pants pockets. "The police asked us to stay out of things until they finished their investigation. And we did. But we should have been in touch before today. Again, I'm sorry."

"It's okay," Rich replied, turning back to the stairs.

"One other thing, Rick," Jen said, standing up so she could look into his eyes. "We've been wondering... did you ever see anything strange going on with Kyle? Or with someone he might've brought home or invited over? Was there anyone at all who might've come here and harassed our son to the point... to the point where he'd take his own life?"

The lump in her throat grew, and she swallowed hard. But she would not break down. She'd cried enough for now. It was time to get to the bottom of what happened and who did this to her only son.

"Honestly," Rick said, "I didn't. I never saw or heard anything strange, and he never brought anyone here. Like I said, he pretty much kept to himself." He placed his hands on his hips and bit his bottom lip. "There is one thing, though. He came home one day with a bullet and a note."

"A what?" Keith exclaimed. "Did you say a bullet?"

"Yeah. He threw it at my girlfriend and me and accused us of putting it and a note in his book bag. First, I couldn't even touch a bullet. We're both completely anti-gun, and second —"

"What did the note say?" Jen asked. "Do you remember?"

Rich hesitated. His fingers fidgeted inside his shorts pockets, and he rocked back and forth in his boat shoes.

"I'm not sure I should get into that," he said, looking at the floor as if the wooden boards would give him a reprieve.

Jen would not, could not let this go. It could be another clue as to who tormented Kyle until her son couldn't take it anymore. She pushed her voice past the aching lump in her throat.

"Please," she begged. "If you remember what the note said, please tell us." Her voice trembled as she held herself back from grabbing his arms and shaking the words out of him.

When he finally looked up, he stared into Jen's eyes and cleared his throat. "It said, *You killed Dylan.*"

* * *

Jen hadn't stopped crying since Rick revealed the note's contents over two hours earlier.

Looking out the Lexus's passenger-side window, she watched tears fall down her cheeks in her reflection. Although they began as tears of sadness, they were now tears of anger. Hot droplets streamed down her face. If they were as scalding as her rage, they'd be burning holes in the car seat where they fell.

"No one other than Michael would write something like that, Keith. *You* know it, and *I* know it. Now we just have to get the police to know it. I'm sick of waiting for them to get their act together and find out who did this to Kyle." *Find out who tortured my poor son to death.* "No one can even figure out who started that terrible website they found on Kyle's laptop. Did the person who put that site up just disappear? But whoever they were, they named it *KarmSucksKyle.com.* It was someone who wanted to hurt him. Someone like Michael Wright. That sick boy thought he was taking revenge."

"Honey, I hear what you're saying. I do. But we can't press charges without any evidence. And..." His knuckles tightened on the wheel. "Ultimately, Kyle killed *himself*. It's getting treated as suicide, not murder."

"Bullshit. Remember that case in Massachusetts you told me about? The news clip you read online about some teenagers who bullied that girl until she took her own life? You read that some were charged with manslaughter. There's something there, right? Some kind of precedence for this kind of thing?"

"It was a news clip, Jen. I couldn't find the actual details of what happened. And it's precedence for a case when you *know* who did the bullying. With Kyle, there's no concrete evidence of who might have done what they did... no fingerprints... no nothing. We don't even have the note or the bullet."

Jen opened the glove compartment and searched for a pocket tissue pack. Finding a half-empty one, she wiped her nose.

"Wouldn't it make more sense that the person who left him that note telling him to take all the pills *also* left the note that claimed he killed Dylan? So it's more evidence against Michael."

"You mean if it *was* Michael."

"Damn it, Keith. Why are you fighting me on this? Who else would hate Kyle that much? No one. He was too nice a boy. You know as well as I do that Michael is the only person we know of who hated Kyle, who blamed him for his kidnapping and also for what happened to Dylan. I would bet that if we had that bullet and note, his fingerprints would be all over them."

Keith sighed and banged his fists on the steering wheel.

"Jen, I am not fighting you. We're both very upset, and I'm just trying to bring some reality to the situation. Probably the note about taking all the pills was still there because..."

When Jen looked up to see why Keith had stopped talking, she noticed a tear running from beneath his sunglasses and down the side of his face. She pulled a new tissue from the pack, patted his tear, and gently touched his face.

"Are you okay, honey?"

Keith nodded and swallowed hard. "Yes." He cleared his throat. "I was just saying that the note about the pills was probably there because that's when he took the pills. He probably threw out the other note, the one left with the bullet, because it was too painful to keep." He pushed down the turn signal lever and exited the highway. "I mean, Jesus, who would do something like that? Who would be so callous and... just so mean?"

Jen took a breath through her nose to help hold herself together. "I think we know the answer to that," she replied.

"Michael was not like that seven years ago, and if it *is* him who did this, if he changed that much, which I still can't believe, he needs a *lot* of help. Much more than seeing a therapist once or twice a week."

"I don't even want to think about what happened to him during the time he was kidnapped," Jen said. "It would make me sick and probably also make me feel bad for him. And I don't want to feel bad for him. What I want is for the person who made Kyle take his life pay for what he's done."

Keith placed his right hand on Jen's knee, giving it a gentle squeeze. He kept it there until they'd reached their home, and he pulled into the driveway.

After turning off the ignition, he said, "I'll get Kyle's things from the trunk, and you just go inside. See if you can get some rest."

"Rest?" Jen said, opening the car door. "I'm far from resting. I'm going to call Penny and see who she went to when they sued that drunk driver. She was a brilliant attorney, and I'm sure she knows a private detective who can get us the evidence we need. Then we'll find out the next steps to make sure Michael Wright spends decades, if not the rest of his life, in jail."

CHAPTER 7

"I think I'm going to do a walking tour of the loony bin tomorrow," Parsons said from the chair facing Justin's desk.

"Please tell me you did not just call the psychiatric unit of a hospital a loony bin," he replied, unable to hold back his annoyance.

"Oops," she said. "Sorry. For a second, I forgot who I was talking to. And I'm just kidding around; you know that. I'm just trying to lighten things up a bit."

"Yeah, I know. I have a lot on my mind right now," he admitted. Justin thought he'd been hiding his dark mood well enough, but he should've known Katy's keen sensitivity would cut through his pretense. "Is there any specific reason you're going there tomorrow? Anyone in particular you'll be visiting?"

"Yeah," she said, checking a text that made her phone beep. "First, I'm talking with Devlin. Something is eating at me about his connection to Malone."

Justin swallowed. "Are you saying you think he did it?"

"Well, here's what I'm thinking: this doctor, your friend, would have been crucial in deciding where Devlin could end up spending the rest of his life. I need to find out more about what Devlin knew, or thought he knew, about how Malone was going to handle his treatment. Did he think the doctor would keep him locked up in the loony... sorry... in the psych unit for the rest of his life? Did he think he was going to get him sent to prison? If either of those is true or if there's something else going on, does he have a person or people on the outside who might do something to Malone?"

Justin's thoughts went directly to Michael, and he stopped himself from tapping his pen on his desk blotter. It would only make Parsons suspect that he was feeling uncomfortable. And he was.

Oh shit. What if Devlin brought up Michael's name during their conversation? It would open up Pandora's box so wide neither he nor Mandy would be able to close it.

"What's going on with the investigation?" he asked Katy. "Do you have actual evidence somebody pushed him?"

"Not yet," she said. "Well, no forensic evidence in the apartment or on the terrace. Just a few white cotton fibers beneath his fingernails, like he might have struggled — clawed at someone's shirt as they pushed him to his death. Or it could mean he just finished putting away his laundry." She sighed. "Obviously, we have nothing concrete."

"Well, that sucks," he said, trying to sound disappointed and impatient to get to the bottom of Berny's death. Of course, he did want justice for his friend — but only when he was certain that Michael wasn't involved.

"I'm also meeting with Devlin today to scare him into thinking he's going to prison until the day he dies. Have you and Mandy discussed pressing charges? I know it's uncommon, but I'd love to see a guilty verdict so he's locked up in a cell instead of living in a halfway decent facility like he is now."

Justin leaned back in his chair and swiveled back and forth.

"Still discussing. Mandy knows the law inside and out. She also knows the rarity of locking up someone with multiple personalities. He told Michael about Dylan ahead of time, but can a jury consider that evidence of premeditation if it's unclear *who* told Michael? Was it Nathan? Devlin, the host? Alex? And who pulled the trigger? *I* know it was Nathan, but he can dispute that and make himself look insane on the stand. We could go through a lot of time, anguish and money only for Devlin to end up where he is right now." Justin sighed, stopped swiveling, and set his elbows on his desk. "And that's why we're still going back and forth."

"I can't even imagine how frustrating it is," she replied. "I mean, I'm frustrated as hell about it, and I'm not even the parent of the. . . "

Justin tapped his palm on the desk. "Victim," he uttered. "It's okay; you can say it. Trust me, that word has been bouncing around my head for way too long. Dylan, Michael, Mandy, even myself. Sometimes it feels like we're *all*. . . "

Katy let a few moments pass. "Victims?" she asked.

Justin nodded, his lips pursed as he tried to hide his sorrow. Then, as though someone tapped him on the shoulder, he looked to his side, then at the clock on the wall. "Wow. I have an appointment in about half an hour that I have to prepare for," he said. "Before I start getting ready, are you going to tell me the *real* reason you came by today?"

She shook her head and crossed her arms.

"Well, aren't you a smarty pants today?"

"I told you," he said, smiling. "I'm in a mood."

"Better get rid of it before your patient shows." She stood up and slid her phone into her jacket pocket. "Other than to say 'hello,' I wanted you to know I'll also be seeing Jade when I go to the hospital."

Justin raised an eyebrow incredulously at her.

"Yes, really," she said. "Jade called me from the ward, asking if I would come to see her about something to do with her mother's death. Which got me thinking about something that I wanted to pass by you."

"I'm listening."

"I have this whiteboard in my office. I use it to help me create connections and patterns between people and situations. You know, like those boards you see the cops use on those TV shows?"

Justin nodded. "You mean the ones with photos taped to them and lines drawn chaotically with a magic marker?"

"Yes," she laughed. "But mine aren't chaotic. I promise. That's the beauty of dry-erase markers. When circumstances change, or I shift my thoughts, I just rub them off and redraw."

Justin leaned forward, wishing he was sitting inside her office at that very moment. It would help him see for himself in what direction her theories were going and if Michael showed up any-where on the board. For now, he'd just have to listen, visualize and keep his fingers crossed.

"Anyway, at the top of the board, under the 'victims' category, I have..."

She stopped talking, looked at the floor, and crossed her arms.

"Dylan," Justin said. "It's okay. Keep going..."

"Yes, Dylan, and also Malone, Kyle, and Jade's mother, Mattie."

"Mattie? Why?" He remembered Jade telling him about her mother's death, but he'd never thought to consider her a victim of murder. What made Katy suspect her death had not been by suicide as it appeared? "That's a little strange, isn't it?"

"Actually, it's not. After Jade's call and saying she wanted to discuss her mother, I got to thinking." She smiled. "And you know where my thoughts typically go. So when I put her photo up on the board, I realized all the victims had one thing in common."

"A connection with, or proximity to, Frank Devlin," Justin said.

"Exactly. Now, we know for certain that he killed your son. We also know that Matthew and Kyle had a relationship. Of course, Berny Malone was basically presiding over Devlin's future, and Mattie lived up the hallway from Devlin. When Jade called, I looked up Mattie's records, and the autopsy showed asphyxiation from hanging herself. But you know the way my mind works, doctor. I find it *very* coincidental that Devlin is thrown in the psychiatric unit with a woman who's been there for years with no cause for concern, and only a few weeks later, the woman is dead."

"Are you saying — "

"I'm not saying anything... yet. Maybe I *loathe* Devlin and want to see him get his just desserts. But I'm pretty good at separating my emotions from my professional judgment. And when I do, it tells me something isn't sitting right. Jade's call just increased my suspicions."

Justin kept quiet, not wanting to ask anything further that might lead her chart lines to Michael.

"The question is, how could Devlin have anything to do with Kyle's harassment and Malone's death — *if* he was murdered — from inside a psych unit? So I need to look at what connections he might have from the outside." Parsons leaned over the desk and glanced around the room as though making sure the walls couldn't hear her. "I had my... I'll call them 'insiders'... check him and his room for a phone. They came up with nothing, which doesn't mean much because he's too smart for that. If he *does* have a phone, he probably keeps it somewhere no one would even think of looking. Still, the search was a start."

Justin nodded.

"I'm hoping Jade can help move things further down the road. So... is there anything you could tell me that might help me while I'm talking with her?"

Justin leaned back and clasped his hands. "You mean something that we might have discussed during our sessions?"

"Yes." Parsons nodded. "That's exactly what I mean."

"Are you trying to get me to lose my license today or a few weeks from now?"

"Justin, please. You know I would never — "

"Katy, you just did." He looked at the clock and stood. "You know I can't divulge any information about my patients. No matter how much I want to find out who did this to Kyle and Berny, the specifics of what went on inside my sessions with Jade are confidential."

Parsons put her hands up as though Justin was arresting her.

"I got it. I got it. I give up. But if anything comes up in the meantime that you think might help this investigation, please let me know. I want it solved ASAP."

"And I do, too," Justin replied, unsure if he actually meant what he said. "I want nothing more than to see Devlin brought down."

"Or whoever else might be responsible," Parsons said as she waved and walked out the office door.

Or whoever else might be responsible. The words echoed inside Justin's head like a burst of gunfire in a hollow cave.

* * *

"Parsons was just here," Justin said, his voice low, as though trying to hide his words from an eavesdropper. Mandy had to raise the volume on her phone to hear him clearly.

"And?" she asked. "To be honest, I have ten folders on my desk I haven't been able to open yet. I probably should have gone into the office today instead of working from home. Bad decision." She sighed. "So unless she told you something relevant to — "

"She told me they found white cotton fibers under Berny's fingernails, and it could be from a struggle, you know, like he was trying to grab someone's shirt as they attacked him. Or, she said, it could just be from doing his laundry."

"And?" Mandy asked again, not sure how else to respond, but with a tightening in the pit of her stomach.

"She's convinced that Devlin is somehow involved with Kyle and Berny's deaths. She thinks he might be working with someone on the outside. If she pursues this, Devlin might bring Michael's name into it." Justin took a shaky breath. "Even if she doesn't find anything, my thought is we shouldn't bring Devlin to court. There's no doubt he'll bring up Michael's name, like he did with me. And it doesn't matter whether what he says is true or a flat-out lie; it would wreak havoc in all of our lives."

"Justin." She dropped a folder onto her desk and sank back in her chair. "We don't even know if Michael *is* involved with anything.

Like you said, Devlin could be making this stuff up just to torment you, like he's been doing since the first day he set foot in your office."

"I know. But let's just hold off on filing any charges until — "

"Until what? Until you have proof that your only living son is not a killer?"

"Mandy — "

"He's *not*, Justin! He might be acting strange, and yes, I admit, I've been concerned about some of his actions. But I know that Michael is the same sweet, wonderful person he was before... before he left. It's just hidden underneath a lot of pain. We'll get him back. I know we will."

She heard Justin let out a sigh. Then another.

"I do too, Mandy. In the meantime, can we just hold off a little longer? I really think it's better to play it safe than sorry, at least until Katy finds another path in her investigation. What do you say?"

"Fine. We'll wait. But the minute something happens that proves *my* sixth sense is correct, and Michael isn't guilty of a thing, we're going to make sure that, one way or another, that piece of shit goes to prison."

"You have a deal," he said.

"I love you," she said. "I'm sorry if I was short with you. It's just one of those days."

"I love you, too," he responded warmly. "And I understand. Now go get back to work!"

Before opening up the folder atop the pile on her desk, Mandy went to the laundry room and lifted the handle to Michael's hamper. She silently prayed she was wrong, hoping to God she wouldn't find the shirt she thought she remembered him wearing the night Berny was killed, the same night he'd walked into town to see a friend. But as she pushed a few pieces of clothing aside, her heart skipped a beat when she saw it crumpled at the bottom of the laundry pile: Dylan's favorite tee, the one with the purple NYU torch imprinted across the back, the only bit of color on the pure white cotton.

CHAPTER 8

Lauren placed her notepad on the table beside her chair and looked Michael straight in the eyes.

"Before we get started," she said. "I need to ask you a question."

"Okay."

"Why did you tell me that your parents were okay with you seeing Anthony when the truth is, you never told them a thing?"

"Wait." He frowned. "I thought everything we say in here stays here."

"It does, Michael. The problem, in this case, is that your parents came to me and accused me of recommending that you see Anthony without getting their permission. And the worst part is, you erased a voicemail message I left for your father. Now, why would you do that?"

Michael picked at the sofa pillow threads, apparently trying to think up a suitable response. Lauren wanted to say something about how Mandy had done the same thing to the same pillow — to soften him up by letting him know how much alike he and his mother were, especially when it came to empathy and compassion. But she decided that now wasn't the time.

"Michael? Please tell me why you would do that," she repeated.

"I want some privacy!" he snapped, almost yelling. "I feel like I'm always being watched. I just want to do something on my own without my parents breathing down my neck."

"Are they breathing down your neck, or are they showing concern?"

He banged his fists on the pillow and sighed. "I don't know. Both, I guess. Either way, it doesn't matter. I want to be able to do things without eyes on me all the time."

Lauren waited for Michael to calm down before asking the next question, knowing it could stir up his emotions even more. "Is that because there were eyes on you all the time while you were being held? Did Alfred Dingle watch every move you made?"

Michael nodded and picked harder at the pillow.

"I don't want to talk about it," he demanded.

"I don't want to talk about it either," she replied. "We've talked enough about him in past sessions, and rehashing that won't do much good right now." She leaned forward and placed her folded hands beneath her chin. "There's something else I'd like to try today. But I'm going to need you to use your imagination."

He stopped picking at the sofa pillow and glanced up. His expression of anticipation and fear hit Lauren in the gut, almost keeping her from continuing. *We have to do this,* she thought. It had worked with many of her past clients, and it was now Michael's turn. She couldn't allow his apprehension to stop her from doing something she knew could help him.

"Okay," she said. "We've talked about your anger, and right now, I see it in your face and hear it in your voice. What I'd like you to do is the breathing exercise we've done before. Inhale through your nose to the count of four. One... two... three... four..." Michael obeyed. "Now hold your breath for one... two... three... Now exhale to the count of seven. One... two... three... four... five... six... seven..." After they repeated this four times, she asked him to close his eyes and relax his shoulders.

"I'd like you to picture your anger. Imagine it in a room or wherever you'd like to see it. Can you tell me what it looks like?"

Michael's eyelids twitched as though being forced to stay closed. "How am I supposed to see what it looks like?"

"Okay. Why don't you first tell me what it *feels* like? Since it's with you all the time, I can imagine you have a sense of that."

"It burns," Michael said, spitting the words like venom. "It burns. It's hot, like those pokers people use in a fireplace. You stir the ashes, and it comes out with a red glowing tip."

"Okay, that's good. Then you're saying it feels like a hot poker to you. *Where* do you feel it? Where is the burning?"

"Right in the middle."

She thought he might show her, possibly tap or rub the spot he was referring to. Instead, he kept perfectly still.

"Below the breastbone? Underneath your ribs?"

"Yeah."

"Above the abdomen? Sort of in that hollow space between your stomach and your ribcage?"

"Yeah, exactly. That's exactly where it is."

"That's your solar plexus. So, now that you know where it is and what it feels like, I'd like you to go inside your body. Bring yourself down your throat and esophagus and right into that spot that burns. Tell me when you can see it."

Michael's breathing slowed down and deepened. He was following her instructions, and it raised her hopes that this exercise would help in his progress. Her own body relaxed when, after a few minutes, he started taking even longer, deeper breaths.

"It looks like an eel. Like a giant red eel sticking to a window."

"Does it have a face, or is it just a squiggly red wormlike organism?"

"It has black eyes. Small black eyes that stare at me. Narrow pupils, like slits, almost like snake eyes, but I don't see a nose or that tongue that a snake has. You know, cut in the middle?"

"You mean a forked tongue?"

"Yeah. I think it has one, but I don't see a mouth, so I can't say for sure."

"What is it doing?"

"Just looking at me and squiggling on the window, leaving a snotty goo behind."

"So, this eel-like creature, squiggling and squirming. Do you feel this is a good description of your anger?"

Michael nodded. "Yeah. Now it's moving on the window. It's like slithering, still leaving that goo. Yuck." He pinched the sofa cushion on his lap, his tension growing as the eel made its way across the window in his mind.

"Is there a door in the room?" Lauren asked.

"Yes."

"Okay. Now it's time to let the anger — that ugly red eel — slither down the window, across the floor, and out the door. Remember to move out of the way if it comes close to you. We just need to let it out of the room. Tell me when it's gone."

She looked from the clock to Michael, who still squeezed the cushion. Then back to the clock. She checked between them while waiting for him to inform her of the eel's exit. Finally, after almost three minutes had passed, Michael nodded.

"It's gone," he said, relief clear in his calmer tone.

"Perfect," she said softly. "Are you still in that same room?"

"Yeah."

"Is there anything on the window?"

"Leftover goo," he said with a look of disgust.

"Now that the anger is gone, can you tell me what you feel?"

His eyelids trembled again, and this time, so did his lips. Tears rolled from under his lashes and down both his cheeks.

"What's in the room with you, Michael? What do you see?"

His lips continued to tremble, and the tears kept coming.

"Michael? Tell me what you see."

He cleared his throat and swallowed, actions she saw more than heard, as his mouth remained closed the entire time.

Then, at last, he opened it. "It's outside the window. It's a... it's dark out, pitch black sky. Except there's a moon in the sky. Big and bright. Well, half of it is. The other half is as black as the sky. It's like a half-moon."

Lauren wiped her eyes so no tears would fall. Throughout her years as a therapist, a half-moon had more times than not represented a sign of depression — a dual experience with half the person illuminated, trying to fight the sadness, while the other half surrendered and remained in the dark. It certainly seemed accurate in this case, based on Michael's crying.

"What are you feeling, Michael?"

"Sad. I'm just sad. My whole body is sad. My head is sad. My fingers are sad. Everything. Everything is sad."

Through all the tears and weeping, Michael had continued to keep his eyes closed, something she needed him to do so his focus would remain on his visualizations. His face had gone still, firm with the determination to get to where she wanted him to go, to discover what was beneath the anger and hatred he'd been feeling for so long. Now it was time to dig down further. She hoped he would keep his eyes closed for this part, but she didn't expect it.

"You're doing great, Michael. Really, really great. We're almost done. We have to dig just a little deeper. The anger and sadness you're feeling are buffers, shields protecting you against fear. It's nice of them to do that for you, but they've become obstacles. We need to put them aside for a little while so you can feel and work with your fear so you can keep moving forward."

She waited for him to respond. Nothing.

"Now I need to ask you to lower the moon. To watch from the window as it sinks below the horizon. And as it slowly goes down, please tell me what you see."

Lauren observed Michael's expression, movements, and clasped hands on the pillow sitting on his lap. He appeared to be doing okay — until his entire body suddenly jerked. She waited to see if he would say anything or explain his sudden movement. He didn't, and then a few seconds later, he jumped again. She leaned closer to him.

"Michael, what do you see?"

Another jolt, like someone pushed his finger into an electrical socket. He didn't make a sound, but his lips fidgeted and twitched, pulling the muscles of the rest of his face until he looked contorted.

"Michael, if you can hear me, please tell me what you see."

"I'm outside. No more window. Black. Everything is black." His voice was weak and trembling. "But there's a face in the blackness. Two giant holes for eyes that are glowing. And its nose — I guess it needs to breathe? — shaped like a white triangle with more black on the bottom. And it has an opening for a mouth, really big, like it's screaming. There's fuzz all around it. It's a screaming face coming at me from the dark."

"What do you feel, Michael? Please tell me what you feel."

"I want to open my eyes. I don't like it here. My body is cold."

"Just a few more seconds, Michael. The face can't get close enough to hurt you. I won't let it. Just tell me what you're feeling."

Michael let out a scream that made Lauren jump up from her chair. She wanted to go to him, to hold him, but instead she let him continue, shrieking and hollering until his voice was hoarse and the pillow he held was soaked with tears.

His breath stuttered as he gasped for air.

"What are you feeling, Michael? What do you feel in the pit of your stomach?" To be heard over his sobs, she had to speak in a loud voice, almost shouting.

"Fear!" he screamed. "Fear! I'm scared! I'm afraid! I don't know what to do!"

His cries filled the office, and at last, Lauren gave in to her urge to move to the sofa and put her arms around the sobbing boy. At first, he jumped, her touch scaring him as much as the terrifying face that had appeared from the darkness in his mind.

"I'm sorry," she murmured. "It's me, Michael."

He opened red-rimmed eyes and blinked at her before laying his head in her lap, where he continued crying.

"I'm scared," he howled. "I'm scared. I'm scared."

Lauren held Michael in her arms and gently rocked him. It wasn't anger or sadness holding him back all these months. It was fear. The fear he must have felt as a stranger's hands grabbed him away from his brother that day in New York City; the fear he lived with those first few hours, days, and weeks he'd been held captive, alone and hungry — and the fear he lived with ever since. The fear of uncertainty: What would happen one minute to the next? Who would touch him? Would he be allowed to eat? When would he get permission to go outside? Countless fears residing inside his soul for the past seven years that dug a hole so deep it became part of who he was.

As Michael's arms tightened around her waist, she continued to sway him back and forth, like a mother holding her swaddled baby after she'd answered its cry for her in the middle of the night.

"Shhh..." she whispered. "You're safe now, Michael. You're safe."

Though she knew it was wrong, far outside her professional boundaries, against her personal commitment to nonviolence, she couldn't let go of the one thought swirling around her head — if Alfred Dingle were standing in front of her right now, she'd strangle him to death with her bare hands.

CHAPTER 9

A lfred Dingle looked up at the small, rectangular barred window. It was the only gap in the gray cinderblock-walled cube, a room in which he felt suffocated from the second the guard locked his handcuffs to the steel bench cuff rings.

The prison guard stood in the corner of the room, arms crossed and staring Dingle down like a leopard ready to pounce. Across from Dingle sat Christopher Hansley, an attorney chosen for him by the court. Since Dingle had barely said a word since his arrest, other than saying "guilty" when the judge asked him how he wanted to plead, he had no idea how this conversation would go, or if this public defender would even acknowledge what he was going to ask for.

"How's the name-calling?" Hansley asked, scratching the top of his ginger buzz cut while placing his elbows on the table. "I know it doesn't matter where you are, protective custody like you're in or gen pop with everyone else. I know the name-calling can be rough."

Dingle agreed, but he wouldn't let Hansley know it. The guy was a dick in a suit who didn't give a shit if they found him shivved to death in a bathroom stall or hanging from a prison guard's belt. He was just some underpaid lawyer acting to care until the sentencing hearing was over, and he could continue his occupational benevolence pretense for someone else.

But he understood how prisons worked, that much Dingle knew from their infrequent time together. It didn't matter where Dingle stood, walked, peed or shat. It didn't even matter if he was sitting alone in his cell minding his own business; the verbal abuse echoed throughout the prison hallways.

"ChoMo!" was the most common. Easiest to say, most humorous to the inmates because it rhymed, he assumed. Plus, he figured it was the quickest way for his tormentors to accuse him of being what they knew he was: a child molester.

There were other epithets they'd hurl at him, terms he'd have to look up online. *Tree Jumper,* for instance, is someone who stalks children and hides in bushes or behind trees. *Short eyes* was another, a term based on some guy named Piñero who wrote a book while in prison and used a pedophile as one of the main characters.

When the name-calling first started, he was desperate to make them realize he wasn't what they believed him to be. He didn't jump out of bushes and hold children hostage to torture them. No, he truly loved each and every one of them and wouldn't do anything to hurt a child.

But he knew they wouldn't understand. The idiots in this place were just that, idiots. They wouldn't — no — they *couldn't* understand that it was his duty to release these kids from the life and people who currently held them hostage. Who better than him to show these children the true meaning of love, companionship and the solidarity friends can have when they share a common interest and source of compassionate and consistent authority?

These children had found him for a reason, a purpose, chosen and led to him by a divine guide. The same deity he discovered as a ten-year-old boy — when he was sealed up in a metal storage container with a shock collar wrapped tightly around his neck. His drunken father, screaming curses at the ghost of the woman who had left him years before, circling the container and banging on it every so often to prove some kind of point. Or, just a way to scare the shit out of the little boy inside.

The muffled shouting was incomprehensible babble, like underwater conversations he'd have with friends in a swimming pool. Nothing the man said made any sense. It was a confusing, chaotic stream of noise that infuriated, frustrated and scared him — all at the same time.

So Alfred would curl up for lack of space, place his palms over his ears and speak. First, he'd talk about the hatred he had for the man circling his prison. Then about his mother, who had found some other guy and left him alone with a crazed lunatic, a maniac who threw him in this prison once a week for a reason he could never figure out. When his hatred reached the point of puking, Alfred continued his gibberish with multiplication tables, gurgling out solutions he wasn't even sure were correct. And then finally, when his mind was void of thought or couldn't come up with new ways to calm the fear, he'd beg forgiveness for some unknown offense he didn't even know he'd committed.

Although coming close to suffocation in the darkness of the container was mind-numbing, it was when the screaming outside stopped that Alfred started to tremble. That was when his father would unlock the bolt, lift the top of the container and pull the boy up and out by his arm.

"Run for it," he'd yell, demanding that Alfred attempt to escape. When the weekly routine first started, Alfred listened to the man and ran past the dilapidated woodshed toward the forest. That's when he'd hear a loud guffaw, and the collar around his neck sent a shock that felt like lightning through his entire body. He fell to the ground, his neck burning and the terrifying sensation of every bone in his body vibrating. He didn't want to stand up, scared his father would think he'd try running away again and zap him. So he kept his butt flat on the ground and grabbed as much of the yellowed Bermuda grass as he could, something to hold on to in case the man pushed the button on the remote and shocked him again.

"C'mon boy, get up. Try it again." Alfred didn't move. He just stared at the man, his stomach boiling with loathing. "I said try it again!" his father yelled.

Alfred didn't move. *Beast!* This time the shock was stronger, deeper and more painful. He clutched the grass harder, pulling it out of the dried-up dirt. He took a deep breath, knowing that if he cried or screamed, his father would call him a wuss or fag, like he always did, and probably shock him again.

"Are you deaf, boy? I said get up and try it again."

The phrase "damned if you do, damned if you don't" rang in the back of his head. Where did he first hear that? Who said it? Was it his father when he bitched about his mother? His mother when she bitched about his father? None of those questions really mattered. He hoped that thinking about something else, anything else, would keep his mind off what was happening at that very moment.

"Damned if you do, damned if you don't," he whispered, scraping himself off the ground to his knees. With his muscles aching and neck burning, he tried to stand, wobbled a bit, then positioned himself as straight as he could.

"What'd you say? I think I heard you say something. You got something to say to me?"

Other than shaking his head, Alfred didn't make a move. There was no way out of this. If he ran, he'd get shocked. And the same would happen if he didn't run. What was he supposed to do?

He glanced over to the container and realized he had no other choice but to run toward it, jump inside and slam the lid shut. As he lay in total darkness and a fresh wave of shocks began, all he could do was pray that his guide would watch over him and that his father wouldn't hear the screams before he finally passed out.

"Hey, Dingle, where'd you go?" Hansley slapped his palm on the table.

Dingle blinked twice and pursed his lips, trying to stuff the memories back into the deepest crevasses of his mind.

"Did I lose you?" asked Hansley. "You looked like you were in a trance."

Dingle shook his head.

"So, I hear you want to be moved into gen pop. No more protective custody. You're asking to make yourself available to even *more* murderers, rapists and killers of all kinds." He glanced at the guard standing in the corner, then turned back to Dingle, looking him directly in the eyes. "I know those kinds of inmates are also in this section of the prison, but at least now you're protected. Your case is extremely high profile. Plus, your offense, *pedophilia,* to be exact, is considered the lowest of the low around here, and that puts a target on your back the size of Texas. Do you have a death wish or something?"

"I'm dead either way," Dingle mumbled.

"Oh," he turned to the prison guard. "He speaks!" Hansley joked.

The guard didn't change his position or expression, but they spoke volumes — the disgust and revulsion he felt toward Dingle. That was just one reason Dingle wanted out of protective custody. Whoever killed him would be greatly rewarded, and he'd rather have some lowlife inmate who had to work for it get the credit than some prison guard who had it easy with all kinds of weapons hanging from his duty belt.

"I only speak when there's something to say," Dingle muttered, his voice faint from lack of use. He cleared his throat and jiggled his cuffed hands hanging from the table's rings. "First of all, I'm not a pedophile."

He heard a huff come from the prison guard, a low growl, like a bear he'd once heard on a school trip to the zoo. Ignoring the zookeeper, who had instructed all patrons not to get close to the cage, he approached the bear and grabbed the bars. That's when he heard its growl, a sound so low, so subtle; Alfred thought he was the only one who heard it. He remembered thinking how the growl scared him so much he would've rather the bear roared or bellowed. It was a sound that made him tremble and chilled him from the inside out, the same sound now coming from the prison guard staring down at him.

For a split second, he thought about trying to explain why he *wasn't* a pedophile, why the acts he'd committed were for the sake of his children, but after returning Hansley's gaze, he realized he'd be wasting his breath. Sure, this guy might have a law degree, but he was dumb as a brick when it came to real life.

His suit and wedding ring were a little too fancy for his position as a public defender. That meant one of two things: he came from a wealthy family, or his wife had money and wore the pants. Trying to justify his actions or illuminate this man on how much better these children's lives had become because of him was like peeing in the wind.

"I'm a dead man anyway," Dingle said, forcing himself not to look at the guard. "It doesn't matter where I am or who pretends to protect me; someone's going to kill me." He moved his hands again, the unintentional clink of the cuffs, steel against steel, making him shiver. "Why should we wait? Let's just get it over with."

Hansley laughed as he turned to the side of the chair so he could cross his legs. The burning inside the pit of Dingle's stomach had become red hot. Why did he even ask to see this putz? Other than calling him a pedophile and stating the obvious fact that he was prime meat for the wild animals that surrounded him, it was plain to see this guy had no intention of helping him.

"You have no idea, do you?" Hansley flicked a piece of lint off the thigh of his pinstriped pant leg.

"About what?" Dingle asked, trying to determine where Hansley's question was leading.

"About real life," he replied.

How ironic, Dingle thought.

"Meaning?"

"Meaning, you kidnapped the son of one of the city's... no, one of the *country's* most esteemed psychiatrists and held him captive for seven years. A psychiatrist recognized for assisting the

NYPD with everything from solving cases to testifying in court. So, for one thing, you're an enemy of the cops. And, of course, you're a ChoMo, which doesn't exactly make your protective custody as protected as it could be. *Plus,* well... you already know how prisoners feel about peds, so that makes the list of enemies much, much longer."

Dingle tilted his head. Hansley's "real life" comment still not making sense.

"I already know all this. What does any of that have to do with the fact that — "

"Justin and Mandy Wright. What do you think *they're* thinking?"

Dingle shrugged, his thoughts whirling. For the first time since this meeting began, he felt his heart beating, thumping, actually. And thumping hard. Either his blood pressure was rising, or he was about to have a heart attack.

"Do you think Justin and Mandy Wright give two shits about what you want? Do you think they care that you'd rather not wait to die because it's scarier not knowing when it's going to happen?" He uncrossed his legs and shifted his body so he faced Dingle. "You kidnapped their son, and God knows what else you did to him, which led to his other son being killed. So here's what I think..."

"I had nothing to do with his other son's death. I was not involved in any — "

"Save it, Dingle," Hansley calmly interrupted. He continued. "Here's what I think. Parents who are put through what you've put the Wrights through have a real dilemma. I'm sure they want you dead, off this planet, not breathing the same air as them or their son. But here's where the problem comes in. They also want you to suffer. They want you to worry every time you turn a corner, every time you eat a meal or take a crap. They want you to live in fear, to experience the dread and uncertainty their son faced for seven fucking years." Hansley took a deep breath and scraped his fingernails back and forth across his skull. He looked up at the prison guard whose grin revealed yellow-stained teeth from ear to ear. "Sorry, I think I got a little carried away."

Dingle rattled his cuffs.

"I think we're done here," Dingle muttered. Not even the one person who had supposedly been hired to help him was on his side.

"I said I was sorry. I'm just trying to tell you that I'll do what I can to get you moved, but don't count on it. You've put yourself at the top of everyone's shit list and dug a hole so deep; no light can get in." Hansley stood and nodded to the guard. "I'll let you know if anything changes."

With that, he grabbed the doorknob, walked into the empty corridor, and was out of sight within seconds. Dingle looked at his own hazy reflection on the steel table and closed his eyes. How many times would he have to bang his head against the table before he gave himself a stroke? Five? Ten? Twenty? And how long would it take for the prison guard to stop him... or would he even try to stop him?

Before he had a chance to answer, the guard was unlocking his handcuffs from the table cuff rings and twisting his arms behind his back to shackle his hands together.

In silence, he and his captor walked down the corridor to his cell. Through the racket of thoughts in his head, he could hear the name-calling, the cursing and the death threats. It was the first time since he'd run away at eleven years old that he longed to be stuffed into the pitch-black container with a shock collar wrapped tightly around his neck.

CHAPTER 10

To Parsons, it looked like everyone was moving in slow motion. Patients swayed sluggishly in their chairs while watching TV; their hands held puzzle pieces in mid-air above the table, hovering for minutes; and whenever someone approached or spoke to them, their reactions were delayed, enough to make one wonder if they'd even noticed the other person.

She supposed it was the drugs they were on. Or the voices yelling in their heads. Whatever it was, the lethargic atmosphere gave her the creeps, as it always did, and she couldn't wait to get out of the building.

When Devlin approached the window-walled visiting room where she waited for him, vivid scenes of the night Dylan was killed flashed through her mind: the bloodstain on the floorboards of Justin's office. His and Mandy's devastated expressions as she interviewed them. She crossed her arms and leaned against the wall, trying to conceal her distress from both Devlin and herself.

After coming in and closing the door behind him, he stood at the other end of the room. For several seconds, he looked her up and down. Then he smirked and nodded.

"So, to what do I owe this pleasant surprise, detective? I feel honored."

The smug tone of his voice, thin lips, and inflated cheeks told her she was dealing with Nathan. Her anger swelled.

"You shouldn't feel honored," she fired back. "I'm not here to say hello or see how you're doing. I'm here to find out what you know about Doctor Malone."

"You're looking good, detective. That V-neck is sitting a little lower than I remember. And those jeans, they fit you like — "

"Shut the hell up before I get security to throw you into seclusion."

"That gold cross around your neck is new. I don't remember it from the last time we met. Have you found God?"

Parsons wouldn't, *couldn't,* let him see how much he was getting to her. She'd already told him to shut up, which probably already satisfied some of his sadistic desires. She refused to fulfill any more. Staring into his eyes, she pretended to throw a dagger with each tick of the wall clock.

"What do you know about Berny Malone?"

Nathan let out a loud whine, like a husband hearing, "I have a headache," for the third time in one week. "Okay, fine. Don't accept my compliments. What do you want to know about the esteemed Doctor Malone?"

"He supposedly *fell* off his sixtieth-floor terrace, but I'm not buying it. I think there's more to the story."

Devlin sauntered over to the chair beside the table. His expression was calm, disinterested. It only made her more uneasy, suspicion gnawing at her gut. "Well, that would be terrible, wouldn't it? But what would *I* know about that?"

"That's what I'm asking you. He was the person who would have had the most influence on your future... and I have a feeling you know something."

Nathan sneered at her. "Seriously? How could *I* know anything? Who do I talk to? I barely get to make any calls. There's always someone standing right by me if I *do*. How would I be — "

"Who do you call?" Parsons asked.

"That's really none of your business, detective."

"Oh, but it is. Don't you get it? This isn't your life anymore. It doesn't belong to you. It belongs to the police department, this psych ward, your doctors, and if things go the way they should, the prison system." She took a breath to keep her irritation and impatience in check. "So don't make me go through the hassle of getting phone records and making you more of a suspect than you already are. Just give it up now and tell me who you call."

Nathan sighed and drummed his fingers on the table. Parsons waited in silence. The game of chicken was by far her favorite because it was a game she'd never lost.

He sighed again and stopped tapping his fingers. "I call the people who manage my co-op. I call my CPA. I call my attorney."

Parsons approached him and leaned with her fists on the table. "By the way, I checked the visitor log and saw you've had only two visits. One was from Kyle Harper."

He ignored her statement and looked elsewhere, as if there was something interesting happening outside the room.

"The other one was Andi Peterson. Who is she to you?"

"Who is she to *you*?" Nathan snapped back.

"She's the woman I'll be speaking with over the next few days. Is there anything you want to tell me before I meet with her?"

Parsons had to restrain herself from smiling when his nostrils flared, and his cheeks became even more bloated. She was pissing him off, and she prayed to God he would explode so she could get him thrown into a padded room.

He closed his eyes and let a few seconds pass before opening his mouth. "I don't think you stalking my friends is a legal activity. You have no right to — "

"What did I just finish telling you? This isn't your life. I can follow you around these halls all day and watch your every move if I want to. I can follow your friends around, too, if I'm in the mood. I can have them rip the door off your bathroom so you can't even take a crap without someone watching you. So don't tell me what I can and can't do, Mr. Devlin."

Parsons was half full of shit, and she knew it. But did he?

"I think I'll call my lawyer and see what he thinks about your threats."

"Be my guest, Devlin. I have a feeling your attorney doesn't give half a shit about your complaints. Speaking of which, does your attorney know the Wrights are considering pressing charges against you? Like most people in this city, they would like to see you in prison rather than living this life of luxury."

Nathan looked around the room and moved his arm in a circular motion toward the Day Room. "You call this luxury? Are you kidding me?"

"It's a lot nicer than an eight-foot by six-foot cell. And I'm sure you've heard the stories of what they do to pedophiles in prison."

Nathan banged the table so hard the security guard stationed near the elevators turned his head and started heading toward them. Parsons held up her hand, letting him know all was okay.

He stopped short, nodded, and returned to his post, keeping his eyes on Nathan the entire time.

"I'm not a pedophile!" he shouted.

"Well, Nathan might not be, but from what I've heard, Matthew is on the edge. You see, there was this video — "

Nathan stood and walked to the door. He put a hand on the knob, but instead of pulling it open, he glanced at the patients sitting in the Day Room and then at the floor. Obviously, he was trying to decide whether to leave in silence or make a dramatic exit with something for her to chew on.

When he turned toward Parsons, his expression gave her goosebumps.

"The Wrights try to put me away; they'll pay big," he said.

She would not give him the satisfaction of knowing the effect he had on her. Through the bile in her throat, she spat out the first question that came to mind. "Oh, will they now? And how's that gonna happen?"

Nathan opened the door and gave her a huge smile.

"Why don't you ask their son?" he asked before sliding out of the room and oozing down the hall.

Once he'd rounded a corner, and she was sure he couldn't see her, Parsons fell into the chair and laid her head on the table. *'Ask their son?' What the hell is he talking about?*

Her thoughts were so muddled, her energy so depleted, she couldn't even find the strength to curse.

* * *

After what she had just gone through with Nathan, Parsons was hesitant about keeping her meeting with Jade. Her head still spun from what he'd said, and if she couldn't center her focus, how could she possibly be of any help to Jade?

Yet the last thing she wanted was to have to return to this unit anytime soon. The atmosphere, the smell, the slow-moving patients. It all made her feel heavy, weighed down.

Throughout her career, she'd been called to murder scenes where bodies had been mutilated, blood stained the walls, or chunks of brain lay splattered on bed sheets. This job had shown her things that would traumatize just about anyone, and yet she handled each case with the ease of slipping on a pair of fur-lined gloves. But this place was far, far worse. Was it just that, with her investigative skills, she could *do* something about a murder, whereas she couldn't about the illness and despair that choked her here? Maybe one day she'd ask Justin for his take on her odd sensitivities, but for now, she had two priorities: getting through her meeting with Jade and investigating Nathan's reference to Michael. At this moment, she wasn't sure which of the two would be the first to give her a migraine.

"Just do it," she muttered to herself as she walked through the door into the Day Room. Glancing around, she searched for Jade while using her sixth sense to remain alert for any sign of Devlin, Nathan, Matthew, or whoever the fu—

"Hi, detective." The voice came from her right. She spun around and felt a wave of relief as Jade gestured for Parsons to follow her to the giant windows lining the room.

She led her to two empty chairs that overlooked the outskirts of Manhattan's east side. As Parsons sat down in the chair on the left, she glanced out the window and, for the briefest of moments, saw beauty in the darkness. Below her, the headlights of cars driving up and down the FDR were like searchlights seeking their way home. Beyond them, lights from the city's buildings shone — golden squares from the office windows of the massive Citibank building, illumination in different shapes and colors from thousands of houses, and LED streetlights along the hundreds of roads running throughout Greenpoint, Astoria, and even as far south as Williamsburg, Brooklyn. For a split second, she could've sworn she caught a glimpse of the Citi Field lights far out in the distance.

"Hey," Jade said, bringing Parsons back from her short-lived respite. "How are you?"

She turned to Jade, and her heart dropped. The once sparkling green eyes of a strong woman had faded with obvious sorrow, surrender, and boredom. Though she knew Jade was guilty of an act that should put her in prison for decades, Parsons's heart didn't seem to care about justice, as it ached with sympathy.

Maybe it was Jade's self-harm, which revealed her deep remorse, or maybe it was knowing how she'd seen her father's throat slit open by her own mother. Whatever it was that caused Parsons's pity to swell, she had only one hope left for this poor woman: that Justin would find a way to keep her in a mental facility rather than prison. No matter how much this place gave her the creeps, it was softer and kinder than a cell.

"I was surprised to hear from you," Parsons said.

"Yeah, I figured that," Jade replied. "I sort of surprised myself when I called. But I thought it through and figured you're the only person who might be able to help."

Parsons switched positions in the chair, turning so her entire body faced Jade. "Before we get to that, I wanted to ask you a question — do you feel like your doctor is helping you?"

Jade smirked. "Gallagher? To be honest, I think he's a drunk." She pulled on her braid and combed its frayed edges with her fingertips. "Not that I blame him. Could you imagine dealing with the people in this place all day?"

Parsons bit her bottom lip to hold back a smile. "You have a point," she agreed. "But I do hope he can help you with what you're going through. Now, let's talk about why you called me."

Jade crossed her legs and gazed at the reflection of her face staring back at her from the window. When, after some time had passed, she looked back at Parsons, the Day Room's fluorescent lights couldn't relieve the half-circles beneath her eyes, almost as dark as midnight.

"Well," she started, "this may sound strange coming from someone like me, in a place like this and with my past. But, I- I think th- that Nathan killed my mother."

Although Parsons' connections had led her to consider this, hearing Jade say it aloud stunned her. She found it impossible to change her expression or even open her mouth to speak. Between the Michael Wright comment Nathan just laid on her and now Jade's accusation, she wasn't sure how to react. Her first thought was to search for the camera that was secretly filming the upcoming documentary titled *How to Make a New York City Detective Quit Her Job in One Hour or Less*.

When she cleared enough of her mind to catch a breath, she asked, "And why would you think Nathan killed your mother?" Her voice sounded foreign and distant to herself.

"I can't stand that arrogant asshole, but he came over the other day while I was in here and sat down next to me. I gave in and answered his questions, listened to his bullshit. Then he started telling me how he and my mother would talk all the time. He said the conversations were halfway decent, and then she would begin repeating herself, and he'd get annoyed."

Jade flashed her eyes around the room to make sure no one was watching them. "I mean, hello!" She twirled her index finger by her temple. "Being stuck in here helped me realize the woman was on another planet. She killed my father and sat next to him, laughing at a sitcom, for God's sake. Did Nathan actually think he'd have life-changing, philosophical discussions with the woman?"

Parson stayed silent, allowing Jade to spew her venom.

"Anyway, we got onto the subject of how she died, and suddenly he had this look of pride on his face. Then he actually asks me if I think she did it to herself or if someone did it to her. A little suspicious, right? So I asked him if he thought my mother could've been murdered, and he said, 'In this place, you never know. Might've been over something as insignificant as a roll of toilet paper.' And that's when I knew he was involved. I mean, the toilet paper reference is a little too detailed, don't you think?"

Parsons agreed, but she didn't acknowledge Jade's sentiments. She needed a lot more information to start a murder investigation into someone already under investigation for murder — at least a *lot* more evidence than the accusation of a confessed husband killer. She looked around for the camera again, or even Nathan grinning in a corner. *They have to be playing a joke on me. This is too off-the-wall to be real.*

"Have you mentioned this to Gallagher or anyone else?" she asked.

"Yeah, I have. No one does anything. Maybe they think I'm making it up because I don't like that shitbag. That's why I called you. I mean, you probably think I'm a little off, too, but you're my last hope to find out whether he did anything to my mother."

"I'll be honest, Jade. When I was doing research on who's talked with Nathan since he came here, your mother's name came up. I did some checking, and that included looking at her forensic report." For a quick second, Jade's eyes lit up. "It records her death as a suicide. *However,* I'll look into it more as soon as I get a chance, and if I find anything, we'll take some action. Does that work?"

Despite the inkling of hope she tried to provide, Jade's frown suggested she was far from convinced that her only potential ally would help, seeing through to Parsons's own doubt. Sure, when she had a minute or two, she'd look into the possibility of Jade's accusation. But discovering anything by talking to Nathan, the staff, or researching the archived records would be like finding a needle in a haystack; or, as it always turned out when Nathan was involved, getting blood from a stone.

"Yeah, that's fine," Jade replied, standing up.

As they started walking to the elevator, Jade glanced side-to-side watchfully. Parsons was about to tell her not to worry about Nathan when she noticed gauze wrapped around her ankles, stained on both sides with dark blood and lighter yellow-brown pus.

When the elevator arrived, Parson stepped inside, turned around, and held the doors open with her arm.

"You should have a nurse check your ankles. I'm not a doctor, but I have a daughter. Pus indicates infection." She was about to let the doors close but couldn't help herself. "Did you do that to yourself?"

Jade turned and walked away. Without looking back, she said, "Thanks, detective. Good night."

As the doors shut, Parsons banged her fist against the wall behind her.

Yeah, this Gallagher must be doing a great job. A really great job.

CHAPTER 11

It was Justin's favorite time of year, both for the weather and for memories.

As he walked from Grand Central Station to his office, the crisp September air put a bounce in his step. The sky was cerulean blue, with brushstrokes of wispy, almost transparent clouds floating across its endless ocean. Red and yellow-edged tree branches danced in the corners of his vision when he looked up.

It all brought flashbacks of his two boys diving into piles of leaves, learning to ride their bikes, heading off to their first days of school. Images that had become mementos, souvenirs he could touch only with his thoughts and the emotions that rose along with them. Today, for the first time in almost a year, they made him happy, appreciative that he had such keepsakes to fall back on.

He unlocked the door to his office and immediately lifted the window shade to let in the sunshine. Richard Davis was his first patient, and he wanted to make sure that light and positive vibes filled the room. If Richard was angry on such a beautiful day, Justin would have his work cut out for him.

Placing his cellphone and leather bag on the desk, he checked his office phone display to see that seven voicemails were currently in the system. He picked up the receiver and was about to go through them when his doorbell rang. Justin glanced at the clock on the wall. 8:50. *He's early. Might be a good sign.*

He opened the door and was instantly disappointed to see the miserable look on Richard's face.

"Sorry I'm early," he said, passing Justin and walking directly to his chair in the center of the room. "If you weren't here, I would've waited. But since you are, we can get started early. That means you'll have more time between appointments."

Justin closed the door and looked at the back of his patient's head. Richard had taken command of the situation, or he would have if Justin allowed it.

"Richard," he started, "your being early is not a problem. However, pushing me aside to sit in that chair and starting our session by telling me how to arrange my appointments *is* a problem."

Richard leaned back and crossed his legs. "I get this feeling you need to be in control, Dr. Wright. Like if you're not running the show, you feel inadequate or helpless or something."

Justin took a breath. "If you'd like to be a psychiatrist, then by all means, get your degree and open a practice. But please don't come into my office and start analyzing me. I'm afraid it doesn't work that way."

Richard didn't say a word, but the anger in his eyes was so unsettling Justin almost wanted to ask him to leave.

"When we're having a session," he continued, "neither of us has, in your words, 'control.' We are having a conversation, a dialogue. I think you're getting the word 'control' mixed up with 'guide.' My job is to guide you and the dialogue we're having to places that will ultimately help you reach your goals. When you enter the office and start guiding *me*, it could lead to failure. To be honest, I've had patients who constantly try to guide the conversation to where they want it to go. Unfortunately, it brings them to a place where they only hear what they want to hear. That's a waste of both our time and the patient's money. I don't want that to happen with you." He paused. "I'm sorry if I droned on. Did any of that make sense?"

Richard smirked and blew his hair off his forehead.

"Yeah, it did. I get it. I'm sorry." He glanced at his watch. "It's nine o'clock. See, now you won't have time between appointments!"

"Funny. Thanks for your concern. Now, when I opened the door, I could see that you weren't happy. Can you tell me what you're feeling right now?"

"Anger, as usual," he said wearily. "It's always anger."

"On a scale from one to ten, ten being extremely angry — and, if you will, hateful — how are you feeling?"

Richard closed his eyes for a few seconds. When he opened them, he looked out the window and then at Justin. "Seven," he said.

"Okay, now picture yourself getting out of bed this morning. Or let's go back even further to when you first opened your eyes. Can you tell me the number on the scale at that time?"

"Two... ish."

Justin smiled. "Okay, twoish. And what time did you get up?"

"Around six."

Justin glanced at the clock on the table behind Richard. "So it's nine-thirty now. Can you tell me when the two jumped to a seven? Or was it a gradual increase?"

"Well, I was at the two mark, and then I walked outside, saw people, and I jumped to a five with nothing really happening. I know that sounds weird, but it is what it is."

"It doesn't sound weird. It sounds like there's an autonomic response to people. Something inside of you changes when you see or come into contact with others. One thing we need to discover is *why* you have this response. What is the root cause, and how can we change the neural pathways so that there's a different, more positive reaction to being with and around people?"

Richard nodded. "Agreed."

"So, you were at a five this morning, and now you're at a seven. Did something happen on your way here, or did the anger rise again with no provocation?"

"Oh... there was provocation, for sure."

"Go on," Justin prodded.

"I walked about a block and decided to take a cab because I didn't want to deal with the crowd. As a cab pulls over, a woman runs over to get it for herself. It pissed me off some more. Then she asks me if I'm going uptown. I tell her yes, but only a few blocks. She asks me if I want to share the cab. Good thing I had my sunglasses on because I think my eyes rolled into the back of my head. Anyway, I agreed. Still better than walking, and I didn't want to get here late. Within three seconds, she's on her phone blabbing to a friend about 'Janice's bra' and 'How could she wear a color like that when you can see it through a white shirt?' and on and on and on. She was talking so loud and just wouldn't shut up.

And *that's* when I went to a *nine* on the scale. I'm only a seven now because I calmed down since the cab ride."

Justin reached for his leather bag and took his journal out.

"Was my story *that* interesting?"

Ignoring his sarcasm, Justin wrote the date on the top of the page and scribbled a few notes.

He said, "I also don't like when people are so disrespectful that they talk on their phones like no one else is around. But what puzzles me is that you were sharing a cab with a total stranger. You're already angry, people annoy you, and yet you share a cab with someone?"

"Jesus, that's not what's important here. It's the anger that I felt eating at my gut every time she opened her mouth. *That's* why I'm here. I don't want to feel that anymore."

Justin also wanted to get to the origin of his anger, of course, but his feeling that Richard was hiding something took precedence.

"I hear you, but I'm sorry. . . sharing a cab is such a rare occurrence. Especially if the weather is as nice as it is today. I mean, if it's raining and two people are running for the same cab, you might decide it's easier to share so you don't have to wait for another one. But on a day like today? You could've either continued to walk or waited for another taxi to show up. But you didn't. Any idea why?"

Richard shrugged his shoulders. "I just said 'yes' and figured it would be over in a few minutes. I was not expecting Gabby McGab to get on the phone and start yapping like a fool."

Justin nodded, not in agreement so much as encouragement for Richard to talk. He asked his next question: "Do you think you might have *needed* to get angry? Maybe five wasn't high enough?"

"You're kidding me, right? You think I *wanted* to get to a nine? I'm here to learn how to decrease my anger. Why would I *want* to increase it?"

"Just a thought here, but maybe having your anger at a high level is *comfortable* for you. It's sort of a security blanket because you're so used to it. I'm not saying you *want* to be angry, and I know it might sound counterintuitive. I'm just saying it's possible that, in some way, anger soothes you."

"I don't like that idea," Richard said. "And your theory is moving me back up the scale to a nine."

Justin didn't usually take his patients' remarks personally. Any time his patients became angry, he'd work with them to find out why. When they'd take it out on him, he understood it was because he was the only person available at the time to unleash their feelings on. But Richard's words, and something deep within the timbre of his voice, slammed like a hammer into his ribcage. It *did* feel personal. And he was afraid that Richard might mean it to.

Knowing the answer to his next question, Justin asked it anyway. "Did you say anything to her? Ask her to tone it down?"

"No."

"If you had said something, would it have made you feel better?"

"I would've felt embarrassed, guilty or both."

"So..." Justin thought about how to probe further while keeping Richard's ire at bay. "And this is just an observation. You'd rather *you* suffer than have the person who is *causing* your suffering experience discomfort. Did I get that right?"

Richard nodded.

"Do you think that's fair to you?"

"No."

"Have you always kept things inside? Never released your true feelings of disappointment or frustration with others?"

"Pretty much."

"Well, since we both agree that's unfair to you, it's something we need to work on. If someone is causing you pain or if someone has hurt you, they need to know. Otherwise, they'll continue doing what they're doing and it'll only, like you said, eat at your gut. Also, it's the only way these people will learn to accept responsibility for their actions. If we can get you to do this, I guarantee that over time your guilt and embarrassment will decrease, along with a lot of your anger."

"So, you're saying they have to pay for what they've done?"

The words made Justin cringe. "Not so much pay as understand that as a human being, you deserve respect and civility. And if they can't provide that, you can either accept it and eat yourself alive or remove them from your life."

Richard cracked a smile that looked as fake as a mask to Justin, then slowly and deliberately bobbed his head three times.

"Thank you, Dr. Wright. I'll definitely keep that in mind."

Justin returned the smile, but his wasn't any more real.

CHAPTER 12

"Mandy," Justin said, "I have Katy on the other line. Do you have a few minutes to talk?"

Mandy glanced out her office door and then at the papers covering her desk. If the detective wanted to talk in the middle of the day, it had to be important. It *had* to have something to do with Michael. And when it came to her son, nothing, certainly not drawing up new client contracts or requesting a continuance, would take priority.

"Do you know what she wants?"

"Not a clue. Just asked if I could get you on the line. She has a few questions."

Her sigh was purposely loud in hopes Justin would hear her dismay.

"I know, honey," he said. " I'm sure her call has to do with Michael, so let's nip it in the bud now so we can bring this thing to a close once and for all. I also think it'll help clear some things up for us."

"You're right. I'm sorry. Let's get this done."

After a second of dead air, a short buzz and then a click, she heard Justin speaking.

"I think she's on the line..."

"I don't hear anything. Mandy, are you there?" asked Katy.

"Yes," she replied. "Hi, Katy." She pressed the speaker button on her phone, leaned back and gazed out the window, the vista clear enough to see a hint of the New York City skyline.

"Hi, Mandy. Thanks for taking some time for me. I figured it would be quicker and easier than having you come into the city and deal with sitting in the station."

Mandy unclenched her fists, exposing clammy palms and trembling fingers. Why would Parsons have her come into the city? What could Katy possibly know or think that would be important enough for her and Justin to meet her at the police station? She leaned forward, looking at that hint of city skyline as if it might provide answers... or reach out and demand them of her.

"Not a problem," she lied. "How can we help?"

"So I went to see Devlin the other night. I wanted to get a handle on what he might know, or not know, about Doctor Malone's death because I — "

"And?" Justin interrupted.

"And nothing. It's like talking to Pinocchio. Except when he lies, his nose doesn't grow; his demented ego does."

"Yeah, I figured," Justin said. "Not sure why you'd think he'd tell you anything... even if he really knows something."

"I wasn't surprised," Katy said. "However, I *was* surprised at something he said when the Wright name came up during our conversation."

Mandy stopped breathing. *No. He can't have —*

"He said that if you try to put him in prison, you'll pay big."

"My God, Katy," Justin said. "He's been saying things like that for almost a year. The same thing, over and over. The same bullshit. Why is that such a surprise? I mean — "

"I asked him, how? How can he make *you* pay big when *he's* locked up in a psych ward?"

"And?" Justin repeated.

"He said, 'Why don't you ask their son?'"

Mandy swung her chair around so she could place her elbows on the desk and cup her forehead with her hand. All she wanted at that moment was to see Justin's reaction so she'd know what to say — if she should say anything at all. Another nightmare on their doorstep. What in God's name did they ever do to deserve this?

She remembered Justin's suggestion from when she told him about her fears a few mornings ago. "Cognitive diffusion," he'd said. "When you get caught up in sadness or fear, put distance between yourself and the emotion. Say something like, 'I notice I'm feeling sad about X.' Just saying those words puts space between you and your feelings. The emotion becomes less severe, and then you can deal with it."

It sounded good at the time, but how the hell could she use it now? What was she supposed to say? *I notice I'm upset because my family has been torn apart? I notice that my heart breaks whenever I hear Dylan's name or think of what Michael might be capable of? I notice that for the past seven years, my life has been more heartache and pain than joy and pleasure?*

Cognitive diffusion, my ass.

Katy broke the silence. "Ask Michael, Devlin said. What could he mean by that?"

Mandy was about to reply, 'Just another way to make us suffer,' but she closed her mouth when she heard Justin's voice.

"I'll assume you were speaking with Nathan?" he asked.

"Yeah, he seems to be the one in charge now. I couldn't even tell you if he still has multiple personalities or if Nathan keeps them hidden beneath his relentless hostility. I guess his new doctor would know. But that's for another time. Right now, I need to know why he would bring up Michael's name."

Mandy waited for Justin to come up with an answer. In the silence, she picked at the cuticle of her left thumb. She hadn't picked her fingernails since high school, and here she was, acting like a nervous teenager. The name "Fatty Patty" rang in her head, reminding her of Alex, and her nail dug into her cuticle deeper and harder. *Stop!* She forced herself back into the moment, grabbed her pen and started writing the points she wanted to get across if she had to answer Parsons.

"Really, Katy?" Justin said. "How can you listen to anything Nathan says? You know it's all bullshit. He's not only a murderer, but he's also a sociopathic liar. He made Michael believe Kyle was responsible for his kidnapping *and* responsible for what happened to Dylan. We all know how ludicrous that is. And now he's trying to get you to believe Michael, of all people, is caught up in this mess. It's obviously retaliation against me for him being locked up in a psych ward that he must loathe every single second he's awake." Justin took a breath. "Where does it end? When do we just start ignoring everything he says so we can focus on the actual facts?"

Mandy thought back to the night Justin told her Nathan said to "thank Michael" regarding Berny's death. If Justin were with her right now, she'd ask if he was the pot or the kettle. *You want* Katy *to ignore everything Nathan says, but* you *believe him when he says Michael was involved in Berny's death. Come on, Justin, make up your mind.*

"Justin, believe me, I hear what you're saying about this guy, and I agree. But I have to follow up any lead that comes my way, no matter how absurd it sounds."

Mandy had picked her cuticle enough to make it bleed. She grabbed a tissue out of the box on her desk and wrapped it around her finger. *Where is she going with this? Why is she —*

"First, I want you both to know I am in no way accusing Michael of *anything*. Again, I have to pursue anything that might be relevant to my investigation. So when Nathan first mentioned Michael's name, I tossed it aside like the other garbage he spews. Of course my thoughts started to wander like they always do, and I kept hearing Nathan's words. Again, no accusations here whatsoever, but it's apparent that there *are* connections between Michael and the people in this investigation."

Mandy bit her bottom lip and squeezed her bleeding finger. *Just say it, Katy! Connections to the victims, right?*

"Connections?" Justin said, fury riding on the edge of his tongue.

Katy hesitated, then pushed forward. "Yes. The primary connection being Nathan. Your son was brainwashed into believing Kyle was responsible for his kidnapping. He despised Kyle, a boy who was tormented to such an extent he took his own life. Then Dr. Malone, the one person who could help send Nathan to prison if he so desired, accidentally *falls* to his death from his balcony."

Mandy squeezed her finger more tightly, the pain helping her move further away from her growing anxiety. "My gut tells me

Nathan is involved. But since he's locked in a psych ward without any way of coming into contact with Kyle or Dr. Malone, he must be working with — "

"Michael?" Justin asked with a ferocity Mandy had never heard before.

"Justin, please. I did *not* say, Michael."

Mandy's ribcage thumped until she thought her heart would break through it. Her hands curled into fists, and her throat tightened. She waited for Katy to continue with words that might help soothe their angst. But she didn't. Although she'd started the conversation off with the claim that she wasn't accusing Michael of anything, the statements she was making now weren't matching her original assertion.

Before Justin could say another word, she picked up the phone and took them off speaker.

"Well, I can tell you the night Berny was killed, Michael was home with us. So that's one thing you can take off your list." She closed her eyes, relieved Justin wasn't with her. She couldn't bear to see his reaction to her lie. Would it shock him? Was she causing a rift between them without him even being present? But wasn't it worth it to protect their son? Ice water flooded her veins at the thought of what his expression might look like right now.

"Wow, that's an important fact to know," Katy said. "Thank you for that."

Mandy could hear the detective typing and wanted more than anything to see the words on her screen. *Maybe I should've gone down to the station.*

"Another thing I'm hoping either of you can clear up is a call I received from Mr. and Mrs. Harper. They said that Michael had access to Kyle's apartment keys. They told me about the video you watched with them. The Harpers think... that Michael somehow got hold of Dylan's keys and was the person harassing Kyle." She paused and then, in a quiet tone, asked, "Is there something you can give me so I can put that accusation to bed?"

Though she would have to figure out a way to defend her words to Justin later on, Mandy stuck to her instinctual guns. Right now, Michael and his future came before anything else — even Nathan's 'pay big' bullshit.

"I guess the real question is, how could Michael do any of these things, especially get into Kyle's apartment, if *we* have Dylan's keys? They're in my nightstand drawer as we speak."

"Okay," Katy replied. "Another important fact to put in the file. Last, there's the bullet in the bookbag. Do either of you know anything about that?"

"What?" Justin chimed in. "A bullet in a bookbag? What are you talking about?"

"Mr. and Mrs. Harper reported that Kyle's roommate, Rick, told them Kyle found a bullet in his bookbag with a malicious note. At first he blamed Rick and his girlfriend. But after talking it through, Kyle realized they were innocent. Rick apparently told the Harpers that he's so anti-gun, he couldn't even *touch* a bullet."

"Again," Mandy said, "how could Michael get into the apartment if *we* have the keys?"

"I'm not saying Michael did anything. I'm just asking about — "

"Yeah, this all makes perfect sense now," Mandy cut her off. "Michael gets out of captivity after seven years, and his primary goal is to follow Kyle around and sneak a bullet into his bookbag.

Come on, Katy. Give me a break. Our son may have a few problems to deal with right now, but — ”

“Mandy, please,” Justin stopped her mid-sentence.

She took a breath, her heart hammering, realizing how far she'd gone in berating their friend. But she couldn't make herself apologize. For a moment, all three of them were so silent it sounded like the line went dead.

“Katy, can you tell us what the note said? The one with the bullet?”

Katy hesitated, then told him, “I'd rather not. Like I said, it was malicious. Nasty and cruel.”

“Katy,” Justin pleaded. “You can't unload information like this and then not give details.”

She sighed. “Alright. It read, *'You killed Dylan.'* ”

Mandy hung up the phone and slammed her palms on the desk with such force people outside her office's glass doors peered in at her with worried looks.

You killed Dylan. Each word was a stab in her heart — for Dylan, because his name had been used to end his best friend's life; for Michael, because his idea of who Kyle was had been so hatefully twisted by an evil psychopath. She swung her chair back around and looked out the window.

Dark clouds were rolling in, covering the sun that had lit this room only minutes before. A storm was approaching, and she had no way of stopping it — just as she had no way of coming up with any more excuses for her son. . . or her lies.

CHAPTER 13

A s dusk fell, Jade tried to remember the scent, the smell of the deepest part of twilight, when day becomes night, and people change as dramatically as the color of the sky.

She stood by the tiny window in her room, filling her lungs with air, hoping the familiar aura of dusk would somehow penetrate the shatterproof glass and help her clearly remember the backyard of the brownstone she used to call home. For just a moment, she could be, if only in her mind, lying in the chaise lounge, drinking her Combier-infused Cosmopolitan, gazing up at the sky lit by an amber full moon.

From the bare-walled room in which she stood, Jade watched the giant orb lift over the horizon like a giant orange pulled on an invisible string. The Harvest Moon, her favorite because of its sunset appearance, occurred nearest to the fall equinox — a time when the season, as well as Jade's mood, grew colder and darker. These sensations would make most people melancholy, but for Jade, they provided a strange sense of joy.

Each New Year's Day, she looked up the dates of each full moon for the next twelve months and memorized them. She'd recite them aloud to herself every morning, ensuring she'd remember these special nights so she could take full advantage of what they represented.

The empty pill bottle she'd swiped from the nurse's station a few weeks ago was already three-quarters filled with lithium, the drug Gallagher prescribed after she faked several episodes of bipolar disorder. It took quite a bit of pretending, but Gallagher was an easy mark, and she was a good actress, so all went as planned. It was the only way for her to get the medication she needed, one that could be crushed fine as sand for quick and easy disintegration and *also* help her accomplish her final objective.

She commended herself for all the nights she'd succeeded in hiding the tablets between her teeth and gums as the nurse who'd brought them left her room. The strategy not only let her maintain mental alertness but also allowed her to save enough medication to pull off the plan she'd started making the day Nathan opened his mouth to taunt her with his role in her mother's death. The bottle was in a small plastic bag inside the toilet tank, between the fill valve and the tank wall. With part one of her plan in place, she felt comfortable moving on to part two. Now it was time to play the odds — and with fire.

Two days ago, she had a ten o'clock appointment with Doctor Gallagher. She'd known he wouldn't be there when she arrived because he was never on time. He always arrived at his office huffing and puffing like he'd just run the Boston Marathon, apologized profusely, grabbed her folder from his file cabinet, and started thumbing through it as though it was the first time he'd seen its contents.

Jade never acknowledged his apologies. Instead, she puzzled over why he was so consistently late. Was he drinking in the bathroom from the stash of booze she knew he hid somewhere in his office? Sniffing cocaine in his car? Playing with himself in the closet of the doctor's lounge? Jade didn't know, and two days ago, for the first time, she didn't care either. The only thing on her mind was to get to his office early enough to search for the hidden booze she'd smell on his breath, the musty stench weakly concealed behind the mint TicTacs he'd pop in his mouth every few minutes. It was probably in his closet, a desk drawer, or somewhere inside his credenza. Once she found it, she'd fill her empty Aquafina bottle with the liquor and slip it into her robe's deep pockets. That would take care of part two of the plan.

When she arrived at 9:50, she looked up and down the hallway. A doctor passed her by without acknowledgment, AirPods securely tucked in each ear and talking to someone invisible. She couldn't help but smile. A medical doctor acting just like Jimmy, the forty-two-year-old schizophrenic who sat in the Day Room talking aloud to no one for hours on end.

She took a deep breath, opened the office door Gallagher would always forget to lock, and headed directly to his desk. Booze wouldn't fit in those thin top drawers except in tiny airplane-sized bottles, so she didn't even bother looking inside them. There was no way this boozer didn't have at *least* a 750 ml bottle stashed in this office. So she started at the bottom, opening a drawer that held green, yellow and red folders hanging from thin metal rods.

After a quick glance around the drawer, she began to close it. As she did, she noticed the folders didn't move. *Huh... whattaya know.* Since there's typically an inch or so between the folders and the bottom of the drawer, she'd have expected them to slide a bit with the motion as she pushed. But the folders remained still, which meant there must be something below keeping them in place.

Jade pushed all the folders to the back of the drawer to expose the neck of a Dewars Scotch Whiskey bottle. *Well, that was quick.* With a small smile of satisfaction, she took the empty water bottle from her robe pocket, opened it and placed the cap on the desk. She glanced at the door.

No one.

So far, so good.

She opened the Dewars and carefully poured it into the bottle. Once it was almost full, she screwed the cap on and slid it into her robe pocket. As she tightened the cap on the whiskey, she heard the familiar sound of Gallagher's shoes clomping, in a rush, down the hallway. She barely screwed the bottle closed and slipped it back in place before he was leaning against the doorjamb, flushed and out of breath.

Jade stood and nudged the drawer with her slippered foot, praying she'd be able to close it by the time he looked up. By good fortune — something Jade never really considered herself a recipient of — it took Gallagher a while to recover and come inside.

"I'm sorry," he said, still struggling for a full breath. "The meeting ran over, and I got here as quickly as I could."

"Not a problem," she replied. He didn't seem to suspect anything was unusual.

He walked to the filing cabinet that stood against the wall and threw his brown canvas messenger bag on top of it. Quickly turning around, a look of panic covered his face.

"Why are you in here?" he asked. "Did I forget to lock that fu. . . that darn door again?"

"Yes, and I thought I'd just come in and wait."

"Why aren't you sitting in your chair?"

After a slight jolt of panic, Jade relaxed when Gallagher unintentionally rescued her.

"Peeking at my photos?"

She forced a laugh, looking at the pictures spread across the credenza behind his desk. "Yes, I wanted to see your family."

"That's okay," he said and pointed to the largest frame at the left end of the row. "That's my wife, Fran, and our two boys, Johnny and Peter." He grabbed a folder from the cabinet and approached his desk. Jade took one last look at the drawer to make certain it was shut. The tightness in her stomach loosened as she hurried to the chair in front of his desk. "I'm surprised I never 'introduced' them to you before. It's important you know me as a person, not only a doctor."

"Agreed," she said, when all she really wanted to do was kick him in his doctor nuts and run out the door.

And now, as she imagined the full moon's glow penetrating her bedroom window and caressing her face, an excitement trembled deep within her. For the first time since she'd committed her first sin by killing William, another would pay for their evil on this night, atone for their wickedness. Finally, another would suffer beneath a full moon, the Harvest Moon, the moon Jade looked forward to all year long.

She stepped into the bathroom, where she pulled the bottles of ground lithium and liquor from the toilet tank and placed them on the sink. Opening each one with a chemist's precision, she poured the powdered medication into the Dewars, then cleaned the inside of the pill bottle with sink water and put it back between the toilet tank and the wall. She shook the plastic bottle to help mix the lithium with the liquor and then grabbed another empty water bottle she'd found in the Day Room and poured in some leftover Pepsi that had been sitting on her nightstand. She placed the bottle of medicated liquor on the edge of the sink. Beside it, she set the bottle with Pepsi and added sink water to it until the liquid inside matched the color of the whiskey. Once they looked identical, she slid one into each robe pocket and made her way to the Day Room.

Halfway there, she spotted Nathan at the end of the hallway walking in her direction. As he came closer, her stomach did a somersault, and she leaned against the wall. She not only wanted to gain composure but also wanted to indulge herself — this was the beginning of part three, the piece of the plan that just that day she'd titled "Moonlight Sonata."

He nodded and passed her by. *What the hell?* She wasn't sure why he'd disregard her like that after their last encounter. Maybe he thought she was mad at him for what he'd said about her mother. Or maybe he was just being his normal asshole self. At this point, the reason didn't matter. She had to get him to follow her directions, or else her plan would fail, and she couldn't let that happen.

"Pssst! Nathan!" she whispered.

He turned around and pointed to his chest. "Me?"

She looked up and down the hallway. "Do you see another Nathan?"

He rolled his eyes. "No, I don't." He sauntered over and leaned against the wall beside her. "How can I help you, Miss Jade?"

"Why are you ignoring me?" she asked, making her tone as sweet and pleasant as she could.

"I'm not ignoring anyone," Nathan replied. "I just thought you might be pissed at me. I mean, the last time we spoke... well... you didn't seem real happy to be talking to me, so I — "

Jade looked into his eyes and slowly batted her eyelashes. *This bullshit better work,* she thought, *or I'm gonna make* myself *puke.* If that didn't work, she'd have to grab his crotch, which was the last thing she wanted to do.

"Pissed? Absolutely not. Quite the opposite, in fact."

Nathan returned her gaze and smiled.

"Really?" he asked. "I thought that maybe — "

"You think too much," she interrupted. "I was actually coming to see you. I have a surprise."

Nathan inched closer until their faces were only inches apart. The look in his eyes gave his thoughts away; he wanted sex, and it didn't matter who gave it to him, even if it was someone who might hate him. Actually, he'd probably enjoy that more.

"A surprise? I love surprises."

Jade's stomach did another somersault, this time from the stench of Nathan's breath. She couldn't tell if it stank from something he'd eaten or if this was how his breath always smelled — she'd just never been close enough to get such a whiff. If she didn't know macaroni and cheese was on the menu that night, she would've sworn he'd eaten a shit sandwich.

She glanced down at her robe pockets so he'd follow her eyes. When he did, she lifted one bottle up so he could see the liquor.

"What the fuck?" he said, darting his eyes up and down the corridor. "Where'd you get that?"

She forced a smile and a few more flirtatious battings of the eyelashes. "Gallagher's a boozer. I found it in his desk drawer and couldn't think of anyone I'd rather share it with."

"I feel honored," Nathan said, his eyes filling with even more desire.

Jade grinned inside. *Hook, line and sinker*. It didn't matter how unkempt she looked — strands of split-end hair dangling over her face, not a drop of makeup, or a robe three sizes too big hanging mid-shin — the guy hadn't had sex in months, and she was his only hope. Now all she had to do was get him to his room without ever having to kiss that stinking mouth or lay a finger on his genitals.

"How 'bout we go to your room, drink some of this and then see where it leads?" she asked teasingly.

Nathan curled his arm so she could loop hers through it.

"Absolutely, madam. I will lead you to my humble abode."

Except for the occasional nurse or social worker walking by, the hallways were desolate. Tonight was the Wheel of Fortune celebrity episode, and chairs had been set up in front of the television since ten o'clock that morning. No one was going to miss that event, not even most of the nurses and security guards. It was the perfect night for Jade and Nathan to walk silently together down the hallway, both anticipating, with bated breath, what was about to happen.

When they reached his room, he guided her to the unmade bed and waited for her to sit before sliding the plastic chair over from the other side of the room. He sat with the back of the chair in front of him so he could cross his arms on top of the backrest.

"So, what's next?" He smirked.

Jade looked out the door, grabbed the bottle with the Pepsi —
she kept it in her right-hand pocket, and the alcohol in her left —
opened it up and took a slug.

"What about me?" he asked.

She wiped her mouth and pulled the bottle out of her other
pocket.

"I have a full bottle for you," she said, a seductive tone in each
syllable. She unscrewed the cap and handed him the bottle. Another glance out the door. Still nobody yet; her luck held. "Let's
finish this fast before someone comes by and catches us. Drink it
like you're doing a shot at a bar." She added just a little more fuel
to the fire. "You have done shots at a bar, haven't you?"

"You're kidding, right?" he asked before covering the opening
of the bottle with his mouth. He swallowed its entire contents in
seconds. When he finished, he wiped his lips on the sleeve of his
robe and let out a huge, revolting belch. He wiped a bead of sweat
from his forehead.

"Does that answer your question about doing shots?" He licked
his lips and shook his head like a wet dog after a bath. "Wow,
I didn't realize how much I missed the taste of scotch." Nathan
pointed to her bottle. "What about you?"

She took the empty bottle back from him, screwed the cap on,
and did the same with hers, then slid them both into the pockets of
her robe.

"I had some before," she said, "and I'm saving some for later.
In the meantime, why don't you get off that chair and come sit next
to me?"

Nathan pushed the chair away and settled on the bed beside her. He touched her knee with his index finger, then put his entire hand on her body and crept it up her leg.

Jade slowly stood and pressed her breasts against his face. He closed his eyes and breathed her in.

"Let's lie you down so I can get on top," she made herself say. "I bet you didn't know I like it on top, did you?"

Before Nathan had a chance to respond, his head fell forward, his chin almost hitting his chest. Jade heard him attempting to speak, but he only got out a few gurgles and mumbling.

"Are you okay?" she asked as his body trembled. "Let's lay you down on the pillow." She got behind him and slipped her hands beneath his armpits so she could pull him where she wanted him to go.

He kept shaking as if he had a fever of 106, and the sounds coming from his mouth were incomprehensible. Not that she cared about whatever he had to say.

Jade patted his face as he tried to focus his eyes on hers. She made sure he saw her grin after an especially hard pat. His expression changed as he gasped for breath, becoming a look of recognition, as if he knew what she'd done and was amazed that he fell for it.

She felt his stomach convulse, and he tried to turn on his side to vomit.

"No baby, no," she said, keeping him on his back. He might be a strong man usually, but in his drunken, drugged state, she could handle him. "That's not allowed tonight."

Before she even finished the sentence, he heaved from deep within. Vomit appeared at his lips, oozed over them and onto the pillowcase. He kept trying to turn over, but Jade pushed against him, listening to the rest of the puke seeping back down his throat. He coughed, and she used his robe sleeve to cover his mouth.

"Keep it in, honey. Keep it all in," she whispered as his coughing became choking and his eyes rolled back into his head.

Once the convulsions stopped, she took the sleeve from his mouth and put her ear up to his nose — wrinkling her own and trying to inhale as shallowly as possible. And she'd thought he smelled bad *before*. There was the faintest of sounds, barely a breath. But she had to be sure, so she pulled the pillow from beneath his head and placed it over his face. She pushed hard, waiting for a struggle, but one never came. Within less than a minute, Nathan's body went completely limp.

She removed the pillow from his face, placed it under his head, and again listened for any sign of life.

Nothing.

She pushed her finger against his neck to check for a pulse. She waited and prayed that the stillness she felt would last. Finally, she released a breath and let herself enjoy a sense of relief. Her prayers had been answered, a triumphant revenge for her mother's death.

Jade looked out the window next to the bed. Its frame cut off most of the Harvest Moon, only its bottom half visible if she stretched her neck far enough. She almost laughed out loud when she realized "Harvest Moon" and "Moonlight Sonata" were both songs, two musical classics she could enjoy in one exceptional evening.

She pushed the chair back to its original location, and before leaving, stepped into the bathroom. Jade went to the toilet paper holder and brushed the back of her hand across the roll.

"Wow, that *is* soft," she said, grabbing the roll and putting it under her arm.

She turned to the body on the bed.

"Thanks for the toilet paper, Nathan... or whoever you were tonight."

CHAPTER 14

Lauren noticed a subtle difference in Michael's face. A lightness radiated from his eyes, and he sat with a sense of ease, a calm she hadn't seen before in the months they'd worked together.

"You look a little more comfortable today," she said. "There's, I don't know, a look of relief — in your demeanor as well as your facial expression. Has something happened I should know about?"

With his hands resting on the sofa cushions, Michael shrugged. "I guess after our last session, I thought a lot about stuff and realized some things."

"Such as...?" she asked.

"Well, I thought a lot about Kyle and things you said...*we* said. I also hear my parents talking when they don't know I'm listening. Plus, I looked a lot of stuff up online."

"And what did you find out?"

"Basically, I should never have listened to Nathan. It was a big mistake."

"So what made you realize that? Was it something specific your parents said? Something you saw online?"

"Well, my father says that Devlin — that's what he calls Nathan — is a so- sosee- seseeo…"

"Sociopath?"

"Yeah. Actually, a so-cio-pathic *liar*. I looked it up online, and it said that a sociopathic liar makes up lies for their own gain. They don't care about who gets hurt."

"Did it say anything else?"

"Well, I remember the words compulsive, pathological and a bunch of other shit."

Lauren wanted to link the words together for him — to fill in the puzzle before she started this particular session. She'd planned on adding another layer to their work today, and, being that it could be more challenging for Michael than usual, she wanted to keep his spirits as high as possible.

"Yes, that's correct. A sociopathic liar can look you right in the eye and lie to you without showing the usual signs that would give them away. And you're also right about the fact that they don't care about collateral damage. They have one goal in mind and will create whatever story they need to in order to achieve that goal. In the case of Nathan, he wanted you to believe that Kyle was responsible for your kidnapping and for what happened to Dylan. Unfortunately, Nathan is the only one who knows the reasons behind his lies, and I doubt anyone will ever find out what those reasons are."

Michael tilted his head and clenched his fists. "Yeah, and now I feel guilty as hell about the way I treated Kyle."

"Michael, you didn't know he was innocent. Over the course of months and months, while you were imprisoned and vulnerable, you were led to believe something that wasn't true. Why would you blame yourself for something that wasn't your fault?"

"I probably should have listened to my parents the first time they told me Kyle had nothing to do with what happened to me or Dylan. But I didn't. I believed Nathan instead. A rotten, no-good liar rather than my own parents."

Lauren smiled at him kindly. "I'll repeat what I said: It's not your fault. Not only were you being told lies by a very convincing liar, but you were also in a vulnerable position. You were being held captive by another sociopath. How could you possibly know what or who to believe?" She leaned back in the chair and crossed her legs. "Let me ask you this — did you ever think or hope that Nathan might help you escape?"

Michael nodded. "Yeah, there were some times I would imagine him grabbing my hand and walking me out of that place. Right past the other kids and Dingle, laughing in his face while he put me in his car. But he never did. I don't know why."

"Because from what I've been told, he has very deep-rooted problems, Michael. But we're not here for Nathan. We're here for you — to help *you* lead a normal and healthy life. Are you ready to get started?"

Michael fidgeted, scratching his head. "Uh oh, that sounds scary. Get started on what?"

Part of Lauren wondered if she should let him bask longer in the peace his Kyle revelation had brought. Since that peace was already mixed with guilt, she would have to proceed carefully, mindful of his vulnerability. But after months of work with Michael, she saw that it was time for him to delve more deeply into the fear he'd revealed in their last session, the fear which had been the source of his negative thoughts and actions.

"Well, first let's talk about what you feel differently inside since your realization that Nathan lied to you and Kyle had always been on your side."

"Other than guilty, you mean?"

She bobbed her head. "Yes, other than guilty."

Another shrug. "I feel happier, I guess. I feel better knowing Kyle was a good guy all along. Just like I used to see him as when I was a little kid. I feel happy that he never tried to hurt me or Dylan. Like I said, I feel guilty, but I also feel relief."

"And that's what I want you to feel after this session, too — after all our sessions. The intention of everything we do here is to help you feel lighter inside and give you more air to breathe. I want us to make sure you get to feel and enjoy all the freedom that had been taken from you for so long. Are you with me on that?"

"Yeah." Michael nodded. "I'll do anything, everything that gets us there."

"Good," she said. "I'm *so* glad to hear that."

Lauren's heart raced, but she didn't change her tone, keeping it as tranquil and soothing as if they'd been discussing the weather. "With that in mind, I'd like to talk a little about Alfred Dingle."

"No way," Michael choked out, shaking his head. "Not him."

"Michael, I'm not asking you to tell me about the things he did or said to you. If one day you feel you want to talk about them, I'm always ready to listen. Right now, however, all I'm asking is that you tell me your feelings when I say his name."

"Duh," he said. "Can't you tell by my reaction two seconds ago?"

"Yes," she acknowledged. "I can see that he brings up extremely negative feelings. What I'd like to discuss is *what* those feelings and emotions are."

"Hatred. I hate him. I hate thinking about his face, his body, his stinky clothes. I hate his bald head and his voice. I hate his smell and that he's still breathing. I hate him. *Hate.* That's what I feel about his name. *Hate!*"

Well, it was certainly a start. But before they could go farther, Lauren had to help Michael deal with what had been brought up. They had to find a way for him to move past, or at least around, the hatred for at least a few minutes so he could unpack the emotions underlying his hatred. Without discovering and working on those particular emotions, the hatred would eat the boy up inside until there was nothing left.

"That's totally understandable," she said. "Totally. Now, can you do me a favor and take a deep breath? Just one long, deep breath."

Michael rubbed his palms together and then grabbed a pillow from the side of the sofa.

"I can't." He shuddered. "I can't breathe when I think of him."

"Then don't think of him. Keep your eyes open and look at me. Or look out the window. Look at the paintings on the wall. Anything that takes your mind off him, for the moment, so you can take a breath. Can you do that?"

Michael met Lauren's gaze, blinked twice and took a deep breath. She held back tears, not only of relief but of gladness because he chose her face, her eyes, as a place of comfort and security.

"Can you take another one, please? And, like always, make sure the exhale is longer than the inhale."

Michael followed her instructions and took several more deep breaths on his own. Some of the tension went out of his expression, and as she watched, his eyes began to glisten with tears.

"Do you feel a little better now?" she asked.

He nodded, scraping his fingernails along the side of the sofa pillow.

"Good. Now let me get back to this hatred you feel. Have you always felt this way about him?"

"What do you mean?"

"I'm asking because we've discussed how there *were* times when he let you walk around on your own for a few minutes. Once at a gas station, another time when you were at a Dollar Store, I think you said. And yet, you didn't run away. Did you hate Alfred Dingle at *that* time?"

Michael peered down at the pillow on his lap, examining the fabric as though it was the first time he'd seen it. She tried to read his expression. A blush crossed his cheekbones, as if his rage had turned to humiliation that she'd discovered a secret he'd kept for so long.

"Michael, there's no reason at all to feel embarrassed or that you've done something wrong. It's actually a very common reaction when children, and even adults, are held against their will."

"I don't get it," Michael said, his gaze glued to the pillow. "Why did I ever like him at all? He took me away from my family. He ruined my life. How come I didn't hate him back then like I hate him now?"

Lauren placed her hand on his. "Can you look at me, please?" she asked, keeping her voice soft and gentle.

He slowly lifted his head, the blush of humiliation refusing to disappear.

"There are so many possible answers to your question, I can't answer it without knowing a lot more about what went on during your time there. And you don't need to give me that information right now, not if you don't want to. What I *can* tell you is that people who have gone through the things that you have experience a vast array of emotions and feelings. For instance, when you were first taken captive, you probably felt threatened by Alfred. A completely normal, rational response. Over time, you became reliant on him for food, clothing and basically your survival. Then — I'm going to assume — he showed you what felt like kindness and compassion, which could have produced positive feelings toward him."

Lauren tightened her grip on his hand as his lips trembled and the tears filling his eyes spilled over. "Does any of that strike a chord with you?"

Michael slowly nodded, his embarrassment obvious.

"This is nothing to be ashamed of. You see, kidnappers like Alfred Dingle try to confuse you. They show you kindness that you perceive as real. That makes it difficult to grasp the negative nature of your relationship. You're being clothed, fed, and you have a place to sleep and, after a time, play. So you might start believing that your situation might not be as bad as you first thought. The mind works in miraculous ways to protect us from things that can hurt us, not only physically but emotionally."

Michael tilted his head in an effort to understand. "Then why do I hate him so much now? Why does the thought of him make me want to puke?"

"Since you've been back with your parents and in therapy with me, you've become more able to differentiate between real kindness and cruelty, what should be and shouldn't be, who truly cares about you and who doesn't. Since you've been away from Dingle, your mind and thoughts are returning to a place that's healthier, closer to reality and further from what they were during an unnatural experience of imprisonment and confinement."

She smiled and gave his hand a few reassuring taps. "I know it's very confusing right now. After having time to think and absorb it a little more, you'll probably have questions. You know you can call me any time, right?"

"Yeah," Michael whispered.

"The most important thing to understand is that whatever you feel or have felt is not wrong. Nor is it anything to be embarrassed or ashamed of. If you feel something, you feel it. Period. Though, to be honest, I'm actually happy that your positive attitude toward Dingle has changed in the opposite direction, even though, of course, this hatred is very upsetting. It suggests, to me, that you're gaining a different perspective, one that brings you closer to a life that you can and should be living. One that has potential and possibilities you haven't been able to imagine for such a long, long time. *You* are in control now. This is *your* life, not Dingle's, your parents' or anyone else's. Your mind and body are free forever, and no one can take that away from you ever again."

Michael nodded, still picking at the pillow fabric. His fatigued expression told her she'd given him a lot to think about. Perhaps a little *too* much.

"Now," she said, "one more small exercise, and then we'll let your mind rest for the day." She leaned forward in her chair and placed her elbows on her knees. "At our last session, we did some visualization. Let's do that again today. But remember, breathing is very important. You must promise to keep breathing because. . . well, you know what happens when you don't breathe," she joked, trying to lighten the mood.

"Okay," he agreed. "Promise."

"Close your eyes and take a few deep breaths. . . in and out. . . in and out. . . slowly. . . as you feel your body relaxing, from the top of your head to the tips of your toes. Let me know when you feel comfortable enough to start."

She looked between the clock on the side table and Michael's face. After almost three minutes, his eyelids were no longer fluttering, and his face appeared relaxed.

"Okay," he murmured.

She took her own deep breath and spoke, making her voice a gentle whisper. "The first image I'll ask you to think of might be uncomfortable, but please trust me, it will be worth it." She paused. "Imagine yourself in a cell, like a prison cell with steel bars that won't open. You walk around the cell, searching for a way out, but there's nothing but a toilet, dirty sink and concrete walls with markings from past prisoners. Are you there? Please nod your head when you are."

His eyelids began to flutter, a sign of distress.

"Remember to breathe, Michael. Soft, slow breaths."

He listened to her direction and took a few deep breaths. After another minute or so, he nodded his head.

"Does this place seem familiar?" she asked.

Michael nodded again, his lips trembling.

"I'm sure it does. It's a terrible, terrible place. *But* I have good news. Look at the back wall of the cell. All the way to the right, there's a small silver button that you missed the first time you walked around the cell. Can you see it?" He nods. An inkling of curiosity showed through his dour expression. "Now I need you to press that button. Just give me a nod when you press it."

His fingers moved slightly, as though he was actually pressing the button. He nodded again.

"Now watch the wall slowly slide outward like a giant concrete door. As it opens, you see the ocean — the waves, the sun, the endless vastness of the sea. Can you see it?" The corners of his lips rose just a bit, and he bobbed his head. "There are birds flying above you. You can hear them. You can see their wings, open, unmoving, yet carrying them through the air wherever the breeze takes them. There are lush green trees around you, and the water is bordered by white sand dunes. Nothing but space and air, fresh air. Walk into the white, soft sand in front of you and fill your lungs with the fresh sea air. Smell the crisp saltwater and the lush trees; feel the openness surrounding you."

Lauren heard him take a breath. Then another. His expression was calm, his body almost limp as he settled on the couch.

"Now, when you turn around to look at the prison cell, it's gone. There's nothing but a shoreline, trees, high dune grass waving in the breeze and a cloudless sky that seems to go on forever. The cell is gone, and you are free. Completely, totally free."

Even as Michael's mouth stretched into a smile, a tear fell down his cheek. Maybe it was the first tear of joy he'd cried in seven years. Something inside Lauren flickered with delight that she could share this moment with him.

"When you're ready, Michael, slowly open your eyes."

Once he did, he appeared a little surprised to see Lauren. "Wow, that was great. I swear I was there. It's weird to be here in this room."

She grinned. "That just proves you have a very vivid imagination. Remember that you can go back to that place any time you want. It's always there for you, especially when you start to feel bad or think about something negative."

He started to run his hand over the pillow again. "It's weird, but... something about this good feeling makes me feel bad."

"About what?"

"Mostly, how I've been treating my parents. I've been shitty to them, and they don't deserve it. I think I need to make up for that."

"Your parents understand why you've been acting the way you have. Trust me, Michael, there's nothing to make up for. Seeing you smile, feel joy and live a fulfilled life is all they need from you."

Michael looked out the window, still picking at the sofa cushion.

"Yeah, but how do I make up for the things I've *done*?" he asked.

Lauren's heart skipped a beat, and the delight that had been kindled inside it was cooled by a rush of uneasiness.

"What have you done, Michael?"

He stood, slipped on his sunglasses, and walked to the door.

"We'll have to save that for next time. I need to see my parents and apologize."

He left her office, and as his footsteps faded down the corridor outside, Lauren sat still, remembering the question Mandy had asked her and wondering if sitting on a witness stand was closer to reality than she thought.

CHAPTER 15

"Where is he?" Justin asked, separating two slats of the front window blinds to see more of the driveway. "He should've been home from Lauren's by seven... eight at the latest. We should call his cell."

Back in the living room, Mandy sat on the sofa, bare feet tucked beneath her, legal documents in hand. "Honey, maybe he missed the train," she called. "Maybe he's walking around the city. Let's give him a few more minutes before calling and acting like helicopter parents."

Justin released the blinds so they fell back in place. He walked through the dining room to the living room, where he sat in the armchair across from Mandy and from the clock showing ten o'clock at night.

"Let's talk about helicopter parents for a second," he said.

She put down the papers and took off her reading glasses. "What about them?"

"The things you said on the phone to Katy today, the flat-out lies to a police detective. That seems to go a lot farther than being a bit overbearing in checking on our son. I know you believe Michael is innocent of any wrongdoing, but — ”

“But what, Justin? You don’t?”

Justin’s stomach clenched. He clasped his hands to release some nervous energy by twiddling his thumbs. “Mandy, honestly. . . I don’t know. I really don’t. But I think we could’ve skirted around the issue a little better. There was no need to lie. I’d rather have heard a few sins of omission or a ‘we’ll check on that’. Saying something like that could’ve kept things open. Instead, you just lied, and I’m really concerned you left us wide open for, well, for some irreparable repercussions.”

Mandy threw her glasses on top of the pile of papers. Placing her feet on the floor, she leaned with her elbows on her knees and looked Justin in the eyes.

“Need I remind you I’m a lawyer?” she asked.

Her sarcasm bit through him like a rusty saw blade, and his face heated.

“I know the repercussions of the things I said. But before anything else, I’m a mother and will defend *our* son until I have nothing left to defend. I believe in his innocence without qualification.”

Justin took a deep breath, letting it out slowly and intentionally loudly so Mandy would recognize his attempt to stay calm.

“I know you do,” he began. “I know how much you love him. I love him, too. You don’t think it feels like a bad joke just *thinking* he was involved in any of this? I just wish I knew where he was the night Berny was killed.” He ran his fingers through his hair and leaned forward to mirror Mandy’s position. “But with Devlin’s bullshit influence on him and the possibility that he might have been in touch with Michael from the psych unit this whole time, I just think it's possible... maybe he..."

"Maybe he what?"

There was no more keeping anything inside. They were talking about their son, their family, and he had to put everything out in the open. He could only hope they'd find out the facts sooner rather than later, but until then, his theories were all he had.

"Maybe he talked Michael into doing bad things. Things we would never think our son could do. The boy was held captive for seven years, deluded by a kidnapper and lied to by a sociopath. It's possible he could have talked him into anything."

Mandy kept her eyes on him as he spoke, her lips growing thin. But then her hand reached for some papers, and she started shuffling them. Over the decades of their marriage, he'd come to know the signs his wife was hiding something. *Oh shit, what?* He took another deep breath and sat back in the chair to make space between them so that what he said next wouldn't come off as aggressive, or accusatory.

"What?" he asked.

"What, what?" she asked back, looking over one of her briefs.

"I know you, and I know your avoidance techniques, sweetheart. Tell me what you know, please?"

Mandy tossed the papers on the sofa and stood. "What I'm about to tell you isn't proof of anything. Remember that, Justin."

"Go on," he said, although it felt like something rattled in his chest.

"The night Berny was killed..." She swallowed.

With his heart beating against his ribcage, Justin held himself back from yelling, *Just say it already!*

"The night Berny was killed, Michael was wearing Dylan's NYU shirt."

"So what does that — oh, shit," he said, remembering the forensic discovery under Berny's fingernails. "Dylan's white cotton NYU T-shirt?"

Mandy nodded.

"Okay," Justin said. *It's still not proof of anything. Surely not.* "Okay, so he was wearing the shirt. *That* shirt. There are thousands of people who wear — "

Before he could finish his sentence, the front door opened. They looked to the foyer, and as Michael walked in from it, Justin forced a smile. From the corner of his eye, he saw Mandy's hand move in a slight wave. But there was something about their son that made him look different from how he had this morning, something subtle and elusive, but Justin was sure, something significant. If Justin didn't know better, he would've sworn their son had something done to his face, a very refined facelift or collagen injections. His heart beat even harder, not knowing if the change signaled good news or bad.

Mandy stood. "Are you hungry?" she asked, kissing Michael on the cheek and heading toward the kitchen.

"Not really," he replied. He sat on the edge of the sofa and glanced at them both. "We have to talk," he said; with such gravity in his voice, Justin hardly recognized it. Mandy held onto the back of the sofa as though she needed its support. After a few moments, she gave in and sat down, taking the cushion farthest away from Michael.

"I think I had a breakthrough with Lauren today. That's why we have to talk," Michael said.

Justin was about to congratulate him when the doorbell rang. The three of them glanced at it and then at each other. Justin stood and went to the front door. Through the left-hand sidelight, he saw someone standing there. When he realized who it was, he got startled, his head jerking back as if to avoid a blow. It didn't keep him from opening the door as fast as he could.

"I'm sorry I'm here so late and unannounced," Katy said, "but we have to talk."

If I hear those words one more time...

* * *

Justin led her to the chair from which he'd jumped up and made sure she was comfortable before sitting on the sofa between Mandy and Michael.

"Katy! What a surprise," Mandy said. "Can I get you something to drink... water, iced tea, scotch? Or are you on the clock?" she half-joked.

"Nothing, thank you, Mandy. Like I just said to Justin, I'm so sorry for coming here this late and unannounced. I have news I had to share, and my phone is dead — bad battery." She pulled her phone out of her windbreaker pocket, along with a cord. "Would you mind if I plugged this in somewhere to charge?"

Mandy grabbed the phone and cord and brought them into the kitchen. Her footsteps were the only sound in the house. For the first time since he'd met Katy, Justin couldn't think of anything to say. Between Mandy's lies that afternoon and his son's urgent desire to talk with them, his mind was clouded with muddled thoughts. He prayed she wouldn't ask to see Dylan's apartment keys.

"Michael," she said, standing and reaching over to shake his hand. "I don't think we've ever met. I'm Detective Parsons. But please, call me Katy."

Michael took her hand. "Hi." His voice held a slight tremor.

"Okay!" Mandy said, shaking up the quiet in the room. "You're getting charged up! Now, to what do we owe this late but always welcome visit?"

Justin heard the anxiety in Mandy's tone and saw the reluctance in her expression. She, like him, didn't want to hear what Katy had to say. But she'd always been a great actress when required in her legal work and, apparently, based on today's antics, a great liar.

"I have some news," she said as she shot a glance at Justin and Mandy. "I'm not sure you'll want everyone to hear it."

Justin turned to Mandy. They nodded at one another, and both smiled at Michael.

"No worries, detective," Justin said. "In this house we are totally transparent. So please, go ahead; what's the news?"

If I don't have a heart attack tonight, he thought, *it's never gonna happen.*

"Alright. Well, I have some good news and some bad news. It all depends on how you look at it. I'll just tell you all of it, and then you can decide which is which." She leaned back and looked Justin in the eyes. "Frank Devlin is dead."

His mouth dropped open. He turned to Mandy and saw her wearing the same shocked expression. When he looked at Michael, the boy's face was void of any emotion. He simply watched Katy patiently, awaiting the next bit of news.

"What happened?" Justin asked, his voice sounding as distant as his ability to grasp what Katy had just said.

"The coroner isn't one hundred percent sure... yet. But once the toxicology results are in, we'll have a better idea of what killed him."

She looked at Michael and closed her eyes for a few seconds. It was easy to see she didn't want to keep talking in front of the boy, but Justin wouldn't have it any other way. His son had to hear everything from the horse's mouth so he'd know it was true and that there were no secrets in the Wright house. If he and Mandy didn't keep secrets from him... maybe he wouldn't keep secrets from him and Mandy anymore.

"They found him on the floor of his room," she continued slowly. "The coroner thinks Devlin had a seizure. Because of the, well, bodily fluids and foaming at the mouth, his initial thought was acute lithium toxicity. "

"That's true," Justin said. Since he knew the risks of every medicine he prescribed, he was familiar with those symptoms. "A lithium overdose can cause unconsciousness, coma, or even fatal seizures. But Devlin wasn't taking lithium."

Katy blinked and offered him a subtle nod.

"We'll get to that in a minute," she replied.

"So," Mandy jumped in. "Is that the good news or the bad news?"

"Like I said, that's for you to decide for yourself," Katy said with a faint smile.

"Is there more?"

Katy looked at Justin again and leaned forward. "Have you looked outside tonight?"

"Yeah, why?" he asked.

"There's a full moon."

"Oh, crap," he said. "Is she okay? But what could she possibly do — "

"What does a full moon have to do with anything?" Michael asked.

Katy tilted her head toward him. "Let's just say that one of your dad's patients does some strange things when there's a full moon."

"I thought the unit improved things after... well, after what happened to Jade's mother. I can't believe they'd let another patient harm herself."

"Well, she didn't harm herself this time."

"Meaning what?" he asked.

"Meaning, even though you're right that Devlin isn't taking lithium, Jade *is*. Seems her med was changed to lithium a few weeks ago and — "

"Lithium is primarily used for bipolar patients," Justin insisted. "She is *not* bipolar."

"That's something I can't weigh in on. It's between Jade and her doctor. All I can tell you is that they're currently testing her blood. If they don't find any lithium, well, one can deduce that she's been pretending to take it and somehow got it into Devlin's system."

Justin laughed in sheer surprise. "Why the hell would Jade want to do that to Devlin? What did he ever do to *her*?"

Katy slid her hands into the pocket of her jacket and took a deep breath. "The day I went to the hospital to visit Devlin, I also met with Jade. There's too much to get into and too much speculation at this point. All I can say is that she told me she thought Devlin was involved in her mother's death, and no one was helping her get to the facts. That's why she asked to see *me*. She thought I might be able to help." She brought her hands, still in her jacket pockets, together so they sat on her lap. "Either I took too long getting back to her, and she couldn't wait any longer... or the full moon put her over the edge. *Or* maybe she had nothing to do with it. What I *will* tell you is that if she did, and you were thinking about trying to keep her in the psych unit rather than a prison cell, I wouldn't waste my time. This would put her away for a very long time."

Justin asked, "Have you spoken with her yet?"

"No," Katy said, "not yet. But after the tox screen is in, I'll probably have to go there *again*." She closed her eyes and shook her head. "Not exactly my favorite place to visit."

Mandy bent her knees, pulled her legs close to her chest and lassoed her arms around them.

"Busy night at the hospital," she said.

"Which is why I'm here, I guess," Katy admitted. "Of course I thought you deserved to hear the news about Devlin. But it could have waited until tomorrow if not for... " She sighed. "My daughter is sleeping at a friend's house, and after everything that happened, I just felt the need to get away from the city. You know, just drive and breathe in some fresh air."

"Katy." Mandy got up and walked over to her. "You know you're welcome to stay here. We have a guest bedroom with its own bathroom. You're about my size. I can give you some clothes to wear for tomorrow. Seriously, I don't want you driving back so late."

Justin rose and stood next to Mandy. "She's right, you know. And she makes the best coffee in the morning. *And* the best toast you can imagine. Like no one else."

Mandy slapped his arm. "Smartass!"

"Bad enough I came here unannounced," Katy said. "I am not going to spend the night."

"If you do, you can have a drink," Justin offered, and he was suddenly struck by a yearning for scotch, shared with her or otherwise.

"I really appreciate the offer, but I have to get back. The toxicology report and blood screen could be in, and no matter what they find, I'm going to have a busy morning."

Justin shrugged and gestured for her to follow him into the kitchen. "Let's get your cell."

He unplugged her phone and wrapped the cord in a circle as he walked her to the front door. As he held the handle to open it, Katy put her hand on his.

"I have another piece of news," she said. "I didn't want to talk about it in front of Michael, but you and Mandy should know."

Justin shook his head slowly and closed his eyes. "I'm not sure we can take any more news, Katy."

She took her hand off his and slid it into her jacket pocket. "Well, you're going to hear it anyway, so it might as well come from me." She glanced around to make sure no one was in earshot. "Dingle is dead."

Justin's heart pounded, and a flash of heat from somewhere inside created a thin layer of perspiration across the entire back of his neck.

"What?" he asked with a sense of relief. He thought for a moment, then asked, "That's pretty odd though, isn't it? I thought he was in protective custody, away from the general population."

"He was," she said, looking down at the entryway rug.

"Are you saying someone inside is — "

"I'm not saying anything because I don't know any details. All I can tell you right now is that he's dead."

Justin rubbed his tired, burning eyes, which only made them feel worse. He shook his head again. "Excuse my language, but this is just un-fucking fair. Sure, I'm relieved that Michael won't have to be dragged through Dingle's trial and that I don't have to worry anymore about Nathan seeking more vengeance against my family. But the thought of two heinous monsters not spending the rest of their life in misery makes me angry." He turned to make sure Mandy and Michael were still in the living room. "I probably shouldn't say this, but I was really looking forward to watching those bastards suffer through a trial and then seeing the look on their faces when they were told they'd spend the rest of their lives behind bars." He followed her gaze to the rug. "This just isn't fair, Katy. It's just not fair."

"I hear you, Justin. I do. And I shouldn't say it either, but. . . I don't know what they went through when they were killed, but as far as I'm concerned, their pain and misery didn't last long enough."

Justin let out a breath. "I have a feeling Mandy will feel the same as I do. Conflicted," he said. "You want to tell her?"

She looked up at him and returned his twisted smile. "Absolutely not."

"Thanks so much." Justin sighed, shaking off the sarcasm. "Before you go, I have to ask you about Devlin's death. *Do* you think Jade could have done it?"

"I have to tell you, the last time I saw her, it was like her eyes were empty. She had no emotion in there. Her hair was tangled, she was disheveled, she was. . . I don't know, just a mess. It got even worse after I told her I'd try to find out if there was more to her mother's death. Like she could tell I wasn't going to do much, that it was ruled a suicide, and that would probably be the end of it. She was just so different from the first time I met her."

"Aren't we all?" Justin asked.

Katy took one last look inside at Mandy and Michael and patted Justin's chest gently with her palm.

"Yes," she said. "We definitely are."

CHAPTER 16

P arsons counted twenty screens lining the wall of the security office, each with such an abundance of activity and movement, her head was on the verge of spinning.

"Don't these come in color?" she quipped.

The security guard sitting at the control desk didn't even crack a smile.

"No, black and white only," he said, his tone as dry as her parched throat after running up First Avenue in seventy-degree heat.

"Yeah," she said. "I figured." She waited. "Withers, is it?"

"Yes, Daniel Withers," he replied as he pushed a few buttons and turned some knobs to bring the cameras into better focus.

"Okay, then. I was told you reviewed last night's recordings. Is that right?"

"Yes, ma'am."

"I'm not sure if you were briefed that I was looking for specific images of Frank Devlin and Jade Walker together. I want to know if at any time — "

"Yes, detective. I was made aware of the review requirements." The lack of inflection in his voice made Parsons wonder, for a split second, if this man was a cyborg the security contractor had installed here.

He grabbed a manila folder from the table next to the security console and handed it to her. "All communication between the two patients is outlined in that document. It shows the time, the camera number — which correlates to its location — and a brief description of the activity."

Parsons perused both sides of the single sheet of paper — camera numbers, locations, the time the image was taken, the activity taking place inside the image and the names of those who were in the image. *This Withers is good. Maybe he* is *a robot.* She wished she had one of him at the station.

"Wow, this is good stuff. Thank you, Dan." But as she read the activity column, disappointment pulled at her. Other than Devlin and Walker stopping to talk in the hall and then walking away together down the same corridor, there was nothing specific that could help with her investigation.

She walked behind Withers and again glanced at the wall of screens.

"That's a lot to monitor," she said, hoping to start a conversation. Withers simply nodded. "I'm not second-guessing your attention to detail, Dan. Not at all. I just want to be sure of what you saw because anything, any *minor* detail, might lead us to the cause of Frank Devlin's death." Silence. "Maybe something in Ms. Walker's hands? Or something Mr. Devlin might have been holding? Or if his actions showed anger or hostility of any kind? There might have possibly been — "

"Detective," Withers interrupted, "a death in this facility always becomes top priority, which is why they called me at midnight to come in. My eye for detail is unequaled, and I've watched those recordings three times." His lips pursed as he held back a yawn, and he shook his head as if to dislodge cobwebs and dust. Robotic or not, lack of sleep probably had given them a home inside his skull. "Trust me, I looked for *anything* and *everything* that might help in this investigation. I watched everyone's actions and then went back and examined recordings that included just the two of them. You can see Devlin and Walker in the Day Room, moving down hallways, stopping at one point and leaning against the wall, talking to each other. Then, as you can see here," he pointed at the monitor to his far right, "they head *toward* his room, but since there's not a camera directly in front or to the side of the entrance to his room, there's no footage showing them actually going in."

He gave in to the yawn. His eyes gleamed with water, most likely burning from so much video voyeurism. "I also questioned some of the nurses and other staff. A few of them said they'd seen them together, but they didn't notice anything out of the ordinary. Just two patients talking." He raised his arm and waved his hand along the wall of monitors. "You are more than welcome to go through them yourself. I can have them duplicated and sent to your — "

"No, Dan. Thank you. I trust your professionalism and attention to detail. Please keep them, though, in case we need them in the future."

"Yes, ma'am."

"Later, Dan," she said, walking out of the security room. As she entered the bright, busy hallway and closed the door behind her, at first she felt like she was leaving a little boy in a closet by himself, with no friends to talk with. And then she thought about how robots would rather be left alone to run formulas in their computer brains than converse with a human being. Maybe leaving him alone in a dark, sterile room gave him more pleasure than pain.

She shook her head. Daniel Withers wasn't actually out of an Asimov story. Her own lack of sleep was making her think funny, and she had to keep her mind sharp to get to the bottom of this.

Her phone started vibrating in her jacket pocket. She pulled it out and read the display: *JAY*.

"Whoa!" she shouted above the din in the corridor, which was loud enough for anyone who overheard it to give her a second look. She continued, "The coroner himself. No assistant this time?"

"No, the one and only. I wanted to share my findings with you."

"What have you got? Is it what I expected?"

"Pretty much. Like I thought, acute lithium toxicity. And I called the hospital to get the results of Walker's blood draw — just like *you* thought, no lithium. Not a molecule of medication in her system. Nada."

A surge of sadness ran through Parsons as her thoughts turned to Jade and the dark future that lay ahead for her. She looked up at the ceiling, leaned against the wall and let out a big breath.

"Is there anything else you have for me?"

"No, that's about it. You made this sound urgent, so I wanted to get you the info as quickly as possible."

"I appreciate that, Jay. And thanks for calling about the blood draw. I owe you one."

"Wait… let me check… I think you owe me… one… two… three… we're at four now."

"Okay, four," she agreed, half-joking but wholly grateful — not just for the favors but for Jay's repartee. After dealing with the robot inside the security room, talking to someone with a personality was a breath of fresh air.

"Well, if you go out with me for a drink, we can drop that number to zero."

"Jay," she snapped, gratitude evaporating. "We discussed this. I owe you four. Now I gotta go."

She hung up the phone without waiting for his response and made her way down the annoyingly packed hallway to the lobby. There were people entering and exiting the front doors, staff and visitors waiting by the elevators and others just sitting in the lobby chairs or couches talking on their phones. Ignoring them the best she could, she tried to quiet her mind so she could make the right decision: go upstairs and talk with Jade or go to the captain with her suspicions and let him deal with it from here.

Though Jay's findings hadn't surprised Parsons, the odd sense of pity for Jade continued to weigh on her chest. The woman was beautiful, intelligent, and, at one time, full of life. Now here she was, locked up in a psychiatric hospital for murdering one man and possibly guilty of killing another. Why? Was it genetic? The lasting trauma of seeing her father's throat cut open by his wife? Or the abuse her father had committed that led Mattie Walker to kill him that fateful night? Whatever the source of Jade's current situation, Parsons couldn't find it in herself to blame the woman.

Might as well go up there, she thought, walking to the elevator. She hit the UP button and crossed her arms. *It might be the last time I see her.*

Jade sat by the windows in the Day Room, feet up on the ledge, drinking from a red plastic cup. Parsons tried to look inside of it as she came over.

"A little early for soda, isn't it?" she asked, pulling a chair from behind her so she could sit beside Jade.

The woman glanced up. The look on her face didn't change. There was no surprise, annoyance, concern, or excitement. Nothing but a stare through eyes that seemed to have been drained of color just as her expression was drained of emotion.

"Brings back good memories," she muttered.

"Of what?"

Jade offered no response other than taking another sip of soda. Parsons was speaking to an empty shell, vacuumed out by anger and hopelessness. For a quick moment, she thought about slipping on her sunglasses and leaving, certain she wouldn't get anywhere speaking to Jade. But she stopped herself, pity and pipe dreams keeping her seated.

"I'm assuming you heard about Frank Devlin," she said.

Jade nodded and took another sip. "Pity."

"Do you know what he died from?" Parsons asked.

"Being an asshole?"

I knew that was coming.

"Actually, he died from acute lithium toxicity. Do you know what that is?"

Jade shook her head and shrugged.

"It means he had enough lithium in his system to kill a horse. And alcohol."

"Poor thing," Jade replied.

"What's interesting, Jade, is that Devlin wasn't on lithium."

She shrugged again, squinting from the sunlight now reflecting off the windowsill.

"But you are."

Jade turned to Parsons. "And your point?"

"My point is, there's a reason you had your blood drawn last night."

"They always take blood around here."

Wow, she's a good liar — maybe because being emotionless made it easy to fake a lack of surprise and concern.

"According to your doctor, you're prescribed one lithium pill a night. And yet your bloodwork didn't show a trace of it. I find that odd."

"What, detective? That I don't take my pills? That I don't want to swallow something that would make me walk around like a zombie all day, not knowing who or where I am?"

Parsons didn't have the heart to tell her it looked like she was already becoming what she claimed she wanted to avoid.

"So, what do you do with the pills you don't take?"

"None of your business," she growled.

"I'm sorry, Jade," Parsons said, meaning every word. "But it *is* my business. And it will be the court's business if your story doesn't pan out."

"Jesus." Jade sounded exhausted. "I throw them out. What else would I do with them?"

Fine. If you want to piss me off, you're achieving your goal.

"I have some ideas," Parsons said, "but I'll share those with the prosecuting attorney."

"Oh, so now you're going to charge me with the death of that asshole? You have no proof of anything."

Parsons leaned on her elbow and tilted her body so she could be sure Jade could hear what she was about to whisper.

"Why couldn't you wait for me to do more research... to find out if Devlin was involved in your mother's death? As small as it was, there was a possibility that your psychological state could keep you in a hospital rather than a prison cell. Now you've done something that erased any hope of that happening. Why would you do that?"

Jade looked Parsons in the eye and scowled.

"You're kidding me, right?" Her voice was loud, as if she didn't care who heard, but the words were unsteady, her tongue fluttering with anxiety. "First of all, that 'possibility' you're talking about was never going to happen. There's no way Justin Wright can keep me out of prison for what happened to William. He might *want* to, but it's not going to happen." She turned away from Parsons and looked out the giant window. "And second, about Devlin's unfortunate demise, do you really think I'm stupid enough to admit to something you're making up in your head?"

Parsons leaned back in the chair. At normal volume, she said, "Jade, last night was a full moon. We both know what you've done under full moons. I know you won't admit to it now, but during this full moon, instead of taking your guilt out on yourself, you took it out on someone else."

"Fuck off," Jade said. "Get lost."

Parsons tried to take slower breaths, deeper ones, leashing the frustration that made her want to gnash her teeth. "Show me your scars from last night. Let me see how you hurt yourself. If I see fresh cuts or bruises, I'll be convinced you're innocent."

"I don't need to convince you of anything," she snapped back.

"C'mon, Jade. Prove to me you hurt yourself, and I'll let this go."

Parsons could barely believe the words coming out of her own mouth. *Holy shit. What has this case turned into?*

Jade took another sip of soda and continued to gaze out the window. Her blank expression told Parsons she was done talking, really done, so she stood and slid her sunglasses off the collar of her shirt.

"Fine. I hope you have a good attorney because you're going to have another big fight on your hands."

Before Parsons could walk away, Jade grabbed her by the wrist and pulled it down so their faces were inches apart.

"Just so you know, detective, murder is painful. It hurts, no matter how much someone deserves it."

She looked into Jade's eyes, waiting for her to say more, but she didn't.

"And are you in pain now?" she asked.

Jade let go of her wrist. Parsons stood up straight and waited for an answer, or any response that might lead to a glimpse of an answer. Why had Jade told her that? Was she opening up? Did she need to confess, just as she'd needed to torture herself in penance for two years of full moons? Or had she decided it was fun to taunt Parsons with these hints? Did it help her shake off the zombie fog and come alive again?

"I'm always in pain," Jade said. "Always."

CHAPTER 17

M andy held up two pieces of white bread and waved them in the air for Michael to see.

"Would you like my famous toast your father was raving about to Katy last night?"

"Sure," Michael replied. "With eggs, too, please."

"Of course." She grinned. "Coming right up."

For the first time in months, Michael appeared to have gotten a good night's sleep. His cheeks had a healthy color in them, and his eyes looked brighter, almost as radiant and clear as she remembered them being seven years before. She was happy she decided to work from home again today. Between the late visit from Katy and the even later conversation with Justin about how the news she'd brought might affect Michael, she was in no shape or mood to travel.

"How'd you sleep?" she asked.

Michael sat at the kitchen island and slid the morning newspaper, waiting there for Justin, from side to side.

"Really good," he said. "Not sure why, but I slept straight through until about fifteen minutes ago."

Mandy wondered if the fact that Nathan was no longer alive had anything to do with it. She didn't know of all the lies he might've told Michael, what he'd done to him, or if he'd threatened him. For all she knew, the simple fact that Nathan existed could have been the reason he'd been acting out and saying things that didn't sound like the Michael *she* knew. Now that Nathan was gone, her boy might feel freer, like a weight had been lifted. The man had damaged their lives in so many ways; it was the first time she'd ever celebrated the death of another human being, even it if was in silence.

Make that *two* human beings. After Michael had gone to bed the night before, Justin told her about Katy's other news: Dingle's death. Immediately, relief swept over her like a giant ocean wave cleaning her soul. Not only was Michael now free of testifying against the man who had taken away his youth, but knowing that such evil was gone from the face of the earth made her feel nothing less than sheer pleasure. She thought about telling Michael the news now, but she didn't want to spoil his mood. Plus, she and Justin decided they'd tell him tonight, so they could be together and support him, no matter what his reaction might be.

She glanced at the egg in her hand, the one she'd almost broken inside her tightening fist as images of the two depraved dead men filled her thoughts.

"Over easy?"

"Huh?"

"Did you want your eggs over easy? Scrambled? Sunny side up?"

"Uh, well, it..."

It was obvious he'd forgotten the different ways she used to make eggs for him. Though she'd made him breakfast since he'd been back, before she had made and served it without asking him how he wanted it, so she hadn't named the kinds of eggs. Back when he was ten, the four of them would sit around the island and play the egg game. Mandy would think of a number between one and ten. Whoever guessed the correct number would choose how she'd make the eggs for all of them. Dylan had a knack for it that was almost eerie. He'd seem to read her mind so often that sometimes she'd have to change numbers to give Michael a chance. Justin would just read the paper and smile, guessing a number he knew would never be correct. When it came to the egg game, it was all about the boys.

"I'll scramble them for you and add some shredded cheddar. How does that sound?"

With a relieved look on his face, Michael let out a breath and opened up the newspaper. "Sounds perfect."

As she sprinkled the cheddar on the eggs, the two pieces of toast popped up. She placed them on a plate and took butter and cream cheese out of the fridge.

"Your choice," she said, sliding them across the island to where he sat. "Just don't get any on the paper. Your father likes a clean newspaper."

He laughed. "I just can't believe people still read these things. The letters are so small. And look at my hands; I think there's ink on them."

"I tell him the same thing at least once a month," she said. "But he says it's like reading a book. He'd rather touch and feel the pages than read on screen."

"But you read your stuff online and on your tablet," Michael spoke in between chewing his buttered toast like he hadn't eaten in days. She was too glad to see his appetite to scold him about table manners.

"To each his or her own." Mandy used the spatula to scrape the eggs from the pan onto the plate beside the remaining piece of toast. She placed a fork in front of him and put the pan in the sink. "Reading is very subjective. Some people like fiction, some non-fiction. Some like fantasy, others like suspense. Many people only like reading paperback books; many others prefer tablets." She sat down beside him and watched him eat. "I say, whatever makes you happy is what you should do."

Michael nodded without slowing down. In less than ten bites, he'd finished both eggs and the rest of the toast. Mandy took his plate and stared at it in awe.

"Did you even chew that?"

He laughed. "Chew what?"

She laughed too, warmth spreading through her chest. For the most fleeting of moments, she felt like she did seven years ago whenever she and her youngest son would act silly together. But as quickly as it came, the moment passed when a nagging question resurfaced in her mind.

After placing his dish in the sink, she leaned against the kitchen counter.

"Last night, you said you wanted to talk, and then Katy showed up. I'm working from home today, so I have plenty of time. Did you want to talk about anything now, or did you want Dad here, too?"

Michael closed the newspaper. He placed his elbows on the island and ran his fingers through his already messy hair.

"No, Dad doesn't need to be here. Plus, I know you have an excellent memory and will repeat everything I say, probably word for word."

"Don't be a smart-ass," she fake scolded. "Now get on with it. I'm listening."

"Well, the first thing is, I'm making some heavy-duty progress with Lauren. She's helping me see and understand things I would have never been able to figure out on my own. She's also helping me *feel* things. I know it sounds weird, but they're feelings like I used to have. Like I forgot them, and now they're coming back. I know, I sound like a lunatic."

Mandy went to her son and rubbed the back of his head, feeling his hair under her fingers. "Michael, nothing you ever say could sound weird, and you're not a lunatic. Please don't think that. Ever. Your father and I want to hear everything and anything you have to say." She let her hand fall on his shoulder and kissed his cheek. "No matter *what* it is."

Michael patted her hand. "I also realize now who Nathan was and the bullshit he fed me for so long. To be honest, I'm glad he's dead."

Mandy nodded slowly, although she didn't voice her agreement aloud.

"And I really feel bad, feel *guilty* about the way I treated Kyle. If I only knew what a liar Nathan was. If I woulda listened to you and Dad, I coulda seen Kyle and maybe. . ."

"Maybe what, Michael?" Mandy said, moving along the island's surface so she could face him.

"Maybe he coulda been kind of a big brother, like Dylan was."

It was like a hot knife had pierced Mandy's abdomen. A sharp, scalding blade that ripped through her stomach and up to her heart. First Dylan, his *real* big brother, was taken away — not only from Michael, but from his entire family. And then Kyle, Michael's only hope for a surrogate brother, also taken. . . painfully of his own volition. How she wished Justin was there to help take the blow. But he wasn't, and she couldn't let Michael see her distress. He was suffering enough. She didn't want him to think he was making her suffer just as much.

"I know, honey, I know." She cleared her throat and swallowed. "But you were in a different place then. You didn't know what you know now. Guilt won't do anything but make you feel bad about something you couldn't control." She looked up at the ceiling for a moment, absorbing the peace of its blank white paint, then took gentle hold of Michael's eyes with hers. "To be honest, I believe Kyle understands. And he and Dylan are together, watching over you and helping you get through this. I am absolutely sure of it."

"I hope so," Michael said. "I really do. I don't want to feel this bad about it forever. It hurts too much."

"I know, baby. It will get easier over time. I'm not saying it will go away forever or just disappear. But you'll be more able to carry it. Just know that Kyle held nothing against you and holds nothing against you now. Do you hear what I'm saying?"

He nodded and wiped away the tear that had fallen down his cheek.

"There's one last thing," he said. "It's kinda big."

Mandy's jaw clenched so hard she feared she might break a tooth. She loosened it as much as she could so she'd be able to ask the question. "What is it, honey? What's going on?"

"Well..."

His hesitation made her entire body seize up. She focused on her breathing. God, how she needed Justin right now.

"I've done some bad things. Stuff I really need to apologize for and come clean about."

Oh my God. Kyle! Berny! Did he really do those things? The thoughts bounced inside the walls of her skull, banging, clanking, thumping. She moved backward until she felt the stool behind her. She grabbed its seat, unable to find the strength to pull herself up. With her mind still screaming and her heart beating like a train pounding down the tracks, she clenched her fingers around the cushion and waited for his confession.

"I- when I was- I-" he stammered, trying to find the words.

Mandy closed her eyes, then opened them slowly so he'd know she was listening. "Say it, honey. Whatever it is, just say it."

Michael's eyes filled with more tears, and his breath seemed to stutter from his lungs. "There was this time I was with Dingle. He made me go into this market at some gas station. It was on the side of a dirt road somewhere. He made me steal stuff cause he said we were running out of food. Cookies, soda, candy. He made me and Anthony throw it in bags and then run out into the car."

Mandy tilted her head, confused yet allowing cautious relief to infiltrate her body. Was stealing cookies something Michael considered bad? *God, I hope that was it.* Was petty theft *his* only worry, while Justin tormented both she and himself with his constant concern about Michael's involvement in Kyle's and Berny's death?

"We did it again, at a dollar store somewhere else, and that time, this woman looked at me weirdly and asked if I was okay." Michael's tears flowed down his cheeks. His nose was running, and he wiped it with his sleeve. "Dingle was with me, and he gave me *the look*. And so I told her I was fine. I lied! I stole shit, and I lied for no reason!" He wiped his eyes with the back of his hands. "After that, he said we were thieves, so we could never go to the police, or they'd arrest us!"

His sobbing was uncontrollable, but he put his hand up as Mandy walked toward him.

"I didn't get to the worst part," he said. "We were in the backyard, and there was a rabbit. Dingle saw us trying to play with it and he made us — "

Mandy went to her son. She nudged his hand down and gently touched the back of his neck. She patted, encouraging him until he laid his head on her shoulder. He hugged her back and wept so hard it took everything Mandy had to help him remain upright.

"Shhhh… it's okay," she whispered, even as rage filled her core. Her body was ablaze with anger at the soulless monster who hurt her son in ways she feared she'd never be able to help him recover. "Nothing you did was your fault, baby. Nothing."

"B-ut - I- could have — " His sobs made it impossible to put the words together.

"You couldn't have done *anything*," she said. "That monster made you say and do things you never would have done on your own." She rubbed her hands up and down his back. "He doesn't matter anymore. You are the same sweet, wonderful, caring person you always were and will continue to be. Don't you ever doubt that. Not for one second."

She continued to hold him as his breathing settled and his crying slowed down.

"Are these the *only* things you've done that you consider 'bad'? Nothing else? I want you relieved of any guilt feelings that you've done anything wrong." Was she asking this question for herself, for Michael or for both of them? Of that, she wasn't sure.

Michael nodded. "That's it. Those are the only things I've done, but I still feel bad."

The tension inside her, the uncertainties, the suspicions, evaporated like mist in a ray of sunshine. Her mother's instinct had been correct. He was innocent of the heinous crimes against Kyle and Berny, the wicked acts Justin was so afraid he'd been a part of.

Michael lifted his head and looked at Mandy.

"Sorry I cried like a baby," he muttered. "It's just the stealing that Dingle said would put me in jail. And all the lying and that poor little baby rabbit that — "

Mandy kissed him on each cheek and held each of his arms, stroking them up and down.

"Honey, if these are the worst things you've done, I'm prouder of you than you could ever imagine."

CHAPTER 18

J ustin closed his eyes and inhaled deeply. He wanted to clear his mind before his session with Richard Davis and hoped a few minutes of meditation might help. He let his breath out slowly, then took in another, visualizing the unwanted thoughts leaving his head, floating across the office and out the window into the tumult of the New York City streets.

Calmness enveloped him, and he opened his eyes to look out the window. It was mid-morning, and the buildings across the street cast pointed shadows on the sidewalk just to the left of his office. If he didn't see Park Avenue and all its pedestrians, he would've sworn he was in Egypt, shadows of the three Giza pyramids crawling their way past his window.

His tranquility immediately vanished when the cell phone on his desk vibrated, and Katy's name filled the display. He grabbed it and tapped the green button.

"Hey," he said. "Thanks again for coming by last night."

"Thank *you*," she replied. "It was so nice to get out of the city for a few hours. You know, to see how the other half lives."

"We're half of something," he joked. "Just not sure of what."

"Did that make any sense?" Katy asked.

"Not really," Justin answered. "I'm just trying to clear my head so I'm ready for my next patient."

"Would you like to talk later?"

If Justin wasn't so concerned with Michael's state of mind and potential involvement in criminal offenses, he would have said yes. He was also curious to learn more about what had happened to Devlin and Jade so he could possibly put a period on *something* in his life.

"No, I'd like to know what you found out."

"Okay, but I'm not sure this will help clear your head," she said. "And I'm walking up Fifth Avenue right now, so it might get a little loud."

"Go for it anyway." He held his head in his hand, awaiting the worst.

"So, toxicology shows Devlin had an extremely high amount of lithium in his system."

"And Jade?"

"Not a trace of it in her system."

"Shit," he murmured.

"*And. . .* it turns out Devlin had a high concentration of alcohol in his system. According to the coroner, it was acute lithium toxicity combined with alcohol that caused Devlin's death."

Justin rubbed his forehead. "How did he get alcohol?"

"We're still working on that. From what the coroner tells me, alcohol concentration varies depending on the amount ingested, timing of meals, the person's metabolism, and a bunch of other variables. They'll be checking his stomach contents and probably his vomit to find out what kind of alcohol it was, which might help us figure out the source. In the meantime, what I *can* grasp is the feeling I got from Jade after my very short and disturbing conversation with her this morning."

Justin turned to gaze out the window again. The shadows had moved slightly, now pointing shadows directly at his office.

"And what feeling is that?" he asked her.

"Guilt."

"Why would you say that?"

"So like I said last evening, there's already the fact that it happened on the night of a full moon. And she'd been suspicious of Devlin. She wasn't giving me much, but just before I left, she whispered to me about how much it hurts to have killed someone. And with timing like that, I find it hard to believe she was talking about her ex-lover."

"Okay, I get it, Katy. But her full moon episodes were *self*-harm based on guilt and self-loathing. Even if she thought Devlin had something to do with her mother's death, I'm not sure she would use her special night to harm someone else. It doesn't fit the psychological pattern."

On the other end of the phone, Katy sighed.

"*Nothing* fits *any* pattern as far as this case goes. Let me ask you a question. Do you know Dr. Gallagher, Jade's shrink — sorry, I mean Jade's *therapist*?"

Justin knew Chris Gallagher and wasn't very fond of the man. During a conversation, Berny mentioned him by name, telling Justin he'd talked with the hospital's head of Human Resources. The staff had complained to Berny about Gallagher's inadequacies. Not only had he misdiagnosed several patients, the word on the ward was that he was a man who couldn't manage his own defi-ciencies, mainly his consumption of alcohol. That was the thought that sent Justin jumping from his chair.

"Holy shit," he said.

"What is it?"

"I don't like disparaging anyone, but Gallagher's a lush, and that's probably where Jade got the alcohol for her full moon es-capade. It's clear as day."

"And how do you know he's a 'lush'?"

"Berny told me." Justin said, "Check with HR. Berny said he had filed a complaint with them."

"A drunk. Huh." Her breathing got louder, making it sound like she'd picked up her pace. "Do you think *he* gave her alcohol?"

"No," he replied. "I really don't see a reason for him to *give* her the alcohol."

"So *she* got it *from* him. He keeps booze on premises?"

"That's extremely possible. I know... I knew Berny very well, and he wasn't the type of doctor to lodge a complaint against an-other psychiatrist unless he had good reason."

"You're good at this, doc. Would you like to take over this case?" Her sarcasm made him smile. "I'm going to have to figure out a way to check on that whole situation. By the way," she added, "your son is a nice-looking young man. How are things going?" His smile vanished.

Justin wasn't sure if she was asking as a friend or someone wanting a piece of information to help with her investigation. Any-thing he might say, positive or negative, might raise her suspicions. Although Mandy's lies turned Katy's theories upside down, she didn't give up easily, and he knew she took everyone's words, even his, with a grain of salt. Katy believed something only when she saw it, not when she heard it.

"He's actually doing great. Making a lot of progress. He still has a lot to process and work through, but we finally see a light at the end of the tunnel, no matter how far away it may seem right now."

"I can't even begin to imagine," she said with such sympathy; Justin felt a lump in his throat. "By the way, I don't think I told you this, but when I was going through the hospital visitor logs, other than Kyle and his lawyer, the only other person to meet with Devlin was an Andi Peterson. Does that name sound familiar to you?"

"Peterson." Justin closed his eyes and thought for a moment. He couldn't come up with anything. "No. Never heard that name before."

"Yeah, I'll add that to the list of things to check up on. I'm not sure what kind of people would visit Devlin, or why. Maybe she — "

"Andy is a she?" Justin interrupted.

"Oh, yeah, sorry. She spelled it A-N-D-I when she signed the login sheet, but her full name, according to her photo ID, is Andrea."

Justin floated the woman's name around for a few seconds. Still no recognition.

"I got nothing," he said. The bell outside his office rang, bringing him to his feet. "Patient's here. I gotta go. If I think of anyone by that name, I'll let you know."

"Thanks, Justin. That might be an important part of this Devlin mess."

* * *

Just as Mandy was hanging up from a conference call, her cell phone rang. She wasn't about to interrupt the flow of her workday with a personal call, but she glanced quickly at the display to make sure it wasn't Justin.

The screen read *JEN*.

Her heart fluttered, and a sharp pang jabbed below her stomach. Neither she nor Justin had spoken to the Harpers since the night Jen accused Michael of harassing Kyle. Mandy remembered the last words she'd spoken to them as if it were yesterday: "If you don't shut this crazy bitch up right now, I'm going to slap her face so hard — " and then Justin had grabbed her around the waist and pulled her to the door.

She wasn't sure if she should answer. Michael was upstairs taking a shower, and her office door was closed, so she had privacy. But did she want to speak to Jen? What could the woman possibly have to say? Either more accusations or apologies. Mandy didn't know how she'd respond to either and wasn't in the mood to find out.

But she couldn't run away from the Harpers forever. And now, knowing Michael was innocent of the things Jen had accused him of, dealing with her friend — or ex-friend — would probably be that much easier.

Mandy tapped the green icon and closed her eyes.

"Hi, Jen," she said, not bothering to add *how are you?* To be honest, she wasn't sure she actually cared.

"Hi, Mandy. How are you?"

Jen's voice pulled at her heart. She heard the still-grieving rawness of it. They shared the same suffering, the same anguish. And something inside Mandy allowed her compassion to overpower her anger.

"I'm okay," she said. "How are you?"

"I think you know."

Mandy wasn't sure what to make of her impassive words. "No, I don't, Jen. That's why I asked."

"We both lost a son, Mandy. So, I think you know."

Mandy cupped the back of her neck and rubbed the budding headache there. *I shouldn't have picked up.*

"It's been a while since we've spoken," she said in as calm, even gentle a tone as she could. "Is there a specific reason you called today?"

Mandy heard rustling and crackling and couldn't tell if Jen was turning over in bed or on a sofa or walking around the house to get better reception. She remembered how after first losing Dylan, she'd lay in bed for hours on end, some days never opening the curtains or turning on a light in the bedroom. Thinking of Jen doing the same made her heart ache for the both of them. She glanced at the papers on her desk to change focus.

"Yes, there is," Jen said. She hesitated and then let out a painful sigh, one that sounded all too familiar. "Because you've been a good friend for so long, I wanted to give you the opportunity to tell *me*, not a lawyer or some in-between person, why I should be certain that Michael had nothing to do with Kyle's death. If you can do that, I swear I will not bring a civil suit, or something worse, against your son. But if you can't, then — "

In the back of her head, Mandy heard Justin's voice: *"Just stay calm."* She knew she should, but her instincts were telling her to strike out at Jen with the savagery of a lioness protecting her cub.

Tears of anger filled her eyes, and she braced her elbows on the desk. "If I was your attorney, *Jen*, I would advise you to hang up the phone immediately."

"And why would you advise that, *Mandy*?"

Jen's tone was goading her, hoping she'd say something that could be brought up in court. Although she knew there was no way in hell this woman's baseless accusations could end up anywhere near a judge or court of law. Mandy seethed, but she forced herself to keep cool.

"*Jen*, if you want to suspect my son, I'll never be able to prove his innocence to your satisfaction. You're only going to believe what you want to believe. And then, the day you realize that Michael never, ever communicated with Kyle and that you have contempt for a boy who has done *nothing* wrong, you'll feel guilty, ashamed and beg forgiveness that you will *not* receive. Since your accusations are groundless, please go ahead and bring us to civil court. It will be the perfect place for me to hold you to account for the harassment and emotional distress you are causing me and my family." She paused, took a breath and held the phone closer to her mouth. "Is there any more advice you'd like me to share with you today, or are we done?"

Mandy heard what sounded like a click and then dead air.

"I guess we're done," she whispered.

She threw the phone on the desk. When she looked up, Michael was standing at her office door, one hand on the knob, the other grabbing the frame.

"Does she hate me?" he asked, his eyes wide behind strands of wet hair.

Mandy stood and walked over to him. She brushed the strands aside. "No, she doesn't hate you. She hates what happened and is looking for someone to blame. How much did you hear?"

"Enough." He tucked some wet hair behind his ears. "But why does she blame *me*?"

She led Michael to the chair in front of her desk and then sat down on her own. Leaning forward, she clasped her hands on the desk, her fingers tightly clenched.

"It's hard to explain, Michael, especially because you're not a mother. You may one day be a father, but a mother? No, you'll never be a mother."

"Guess not." His smile let her breathe just a bit easier.

"Mothers often think their sons are perfect — like they can do no wrong. And even if they *do* something wrong, they'll rationalize or try to find someone else to find fault with."

Michael's head tilted, and he brushed his hair back with his fingers as if repeating Mandy's touch. "What does that have to do with Kyle? With Jen hating me?"

"I already told you, Jen does not hate *you*. She hates what happened to Kyle and is trying to find out why he did what he did. She refuses to believe that anyone has anything against Kyle. She wants to think that he was loved by everyone and could do no wrong. No one except for Kyle knows if that's true. But Jen knows you used to blame Kyle for what happened to you. She knows that you once felt he had something to do with Dylan's death. So right now, you're the only one she can think of to point a finger at." She slid her hands off the desk and laid them on her lap. "Obviously you heard enough of our conversation to know that I told her once this is all figured out, she will see that she was wrong. You had nothing to do with what happened to Kyle, and she will regret ever bringing your name up."

Michael looked at his own lap, where his fingers fidgeted and twirled around one another.

"But now you guys won't be friends anymore. They were like your best friends. And now, because I thought wrong things about Kyle, you and Dad lost friends."

"Honey, Jen is suffering. She's lashing out. I've been there; I know what it's like. You yell at people you don't mean to yell at. . . you despise anyone who you think looks at you the wrong way. . . you blame God, the universe, even yourself for what happened. It's a process she's going through, and I understand it completely. The reason our friendship is over is that she's lashing out at *you*."

She reached her hand across the desk with her palm up. Michael took it, gripping firmly.

"She can attack anyone else she wants, even *me* or *Dad*. I can take that in stride because I understand her feelings. But *never* my son. That is the one thing in the world I will not allow."

He rubbed his thumb along her palm. "Thanks, Mom."

She smiled and returned his caress. "There's no need to ever thank me, Michael. I'm your mother and will do whatever it takes to protect you."

Michael looked at her and tensed his lips so the corners of his mouth rose ever so slightly. "But I'm seventeen."

Mandy laughed and squeezed his hand. "I don't care if you're one hundred and seventeen. You'll always be my son."

He shook his head and shrugged his shoulders.

"You'll understand when you're a mother," she joked.

"But I'll never be a mother!"

"Exactly." He smiled at her as she laughed. "Exactly."

CHAPTER 19

Why the hell are you still with him? Andi asked herself. *And why in God's name would you let him move in?*

She looked around her apartment. The sun's reflection bounced off the two-tone bronze octagonal wall mirror she'd just hung, forcing her to squint and cover her eyes with both hands.

"Shit!" she yelled. "Couldn't wait for the window treatments, could you? No. You had to hang the mirror first. What the hell is. . ."

When it hit her she was having a conversation with herself aloud, she shook her head and grabbed her phone off the kitchen counter to check the status of the curtain order.

Stop talking to yourself. Oh shit, there you go again. Seriously, what is wrong with you?

Andi was scrolling through her emails to find the receipt from the window treatment company when her eyes settled on Rick's moving boxes piled high in the empty dining area. It was then she realized sunlight was the least of her problems.

She fell onto the sofa, curled her legs beneath her, and changed the phone's view from her emails to contacts.

She let out a sigh that almost made her choke. Photos of one loser after another, each ex-boyfriend more trouble and heartache than the next. She bit her bottom lip and closed her eyes.

Why hadn't she learned her lesson by now? Was she a masochist? Did she intentionally search out broken men so she could fix them? It was a question she'd asked herself again and again with an answer as hidden as the place people's thoughts go long after they're forgotten.

Andi's mind wandered back to Jason, her high school sweetheart who, during senior year, had two lovers: she and alcohol. He'd never admit his overindulgence, always responding to her accusations with, "I have it under control" or "Andi, stop the nagging. I'm fine."

But he wasn't. And he proved it the night before Senior Prom when they left a friend's house party, and she begged him not to get behind the wheel. Repeating his favorite "Andi, stop the nagging!" he pushed down on the gas pedal and revved the engine in a show of force — and anger. She refused to get into the car with him, and so he took off, leaving her in the street, embarrassed, alone, and praying he'd be okay.

Her best friend Tania listened to her scream, cry and scream some more for almost an hour before dropping her off at home. Walking up the steps to the front door, she took out her keys and, with her hands still shaking with adrenaline, dropped them on the stoop.

That's when her cell phone rang and the display read "UN-KNOWN." Though she didn't know who it was, the sharp bite inside the pit of her stomach told her that the prayers she silently said hadn't been answered.

"Do you know a Jason Moore?" a male voice asked loudly over the sound of sirens.

Please God, no. Please. I beg you.

"Yes... Yes, I do," she replied, her trembling voice sounding as if it came from somewhere distant, out of someone else's mouth.

"He was in an automobile accident. A few broken bones and a head injury, but he's asking for you. He's at Central General if you want to see him."

She tried to gather her thoughts. Should she ask any questions or just get in the car and go there? The officer sounded gruff and somewhat angry, but she had only one question to ask, so she decided to take her chances.

"Can you tell me what happened? Did he — "

"DWI, ma'am. That's all I can tell you. Like I said, you want to see him; he's in the ER at Central General. I have to go now."

Before she could offer a thank you or goodbye, the line went dead. She picked up her keys from the stoop and headed toward the garage to get her car. As she pressed the button to start it, she promised herself that if he didn't get help and stop putting his life — and hers — in danger, she'd end their relationship once and for all.

But a broken collarbone, two fractured ribs, the threat of a breakup and a suspended license weren't enough to stop Jason from sucking down the whiskey like soda pop. And though he tried and told Andi time and again he loved her more than anything in the world, it turned out that the "anything" did not include liquor. It took another DWI and a night spent in jail for her to finally leave him, embarrassed and alone, the way he'd left her in the middle of the street just a few months before.

When she first started her undergraduate classes at Hofstra University's Zarb School of Business, her romantic life was like an instant replay of high school. Guys who enjoyed drinking and partying more than being with her; blind dates that bored her to literal tears from her own yawns; and a liaison with a calculus professor who, after one month, promised her he'd leave his wife if they could make love while she wore a mask and strangled him with a leather strap.

That's when she took a break from searching for love and focused solely on getting her business degree. Without the added pressure of trying to find the "right guy" and going on dates she knew she'd only have to suffer through, she started doing better in school to the point of being able to get her four-year degree in three.

And then she met Tristan. It was her final semester, and her hopes were limitless — for both her career and love life. Tristan, she'd decided after two weeks of dating, was her soulmate. Was it the psychic she'd seen a year before who described her kindred soul as a man with dark skin, thick black hair and chocolate-brown eyes whose name started with a "P" or "T"? Or was it the way her body trembled when he touched her or how his heated whispers sent chills to places within her body she never knew existed?

Andi didn't really know, nor did she care. Tristan was very intelligent and on track to becoming a high flier, meeting with three of the big eight accounting firms and getting offers from them all. His brains, body, potential and sexual skill were only four of the many boxes he checked for her, and she had no doubt that once college was over, the knot would be tied. That was until she came home unexpectedly from a canceled class and saw Tristan buttoning up his shirt as he closed the door to her roommate Ava's bedroom.

When he looked up and saw her, he opened his mouth to speak, but nothing came out. It was the first time she'd seen him speechless, and she wondered if his body felt as numb, his mind as chaotic, or his heart as pained as hers. A wave of nausea hit her when she realized the look on his face said, "no."

She marched right past him to her room, slammed the door shut and leaned her back up against its panels. It took every ounce of energy she had not to reach for the doorknob and let him in as he pleaded with her to let him explain.

Locking the door, she fell onto her bed and sobbed for hours, dismissing Ava's later knocks on her door and endless texts. For the remainder of the school year, she never spoke another word to either of them. Whether it was Ava at home or Tristan on campus, she'd ignore them, acting as if neither of them existed. It was the only way to avoid the unfathomable disappointment and escape the indescribable hurt. She'd never let that happen again, promising herself that *she* came first, no matter who tried to get in front of her.

"I come first," she'd say aloud every morning, breathing deeply while lightly patting her chest. It was a contract she made with herself to protect not only her heart, but her self-worth, as well.

And it worked — until she met Rick.

Andi thought she had smartened up, determined never again to fall head over heels for someone because of their looks, sexual expertise or career potential. She'd decided what was *inside* of someone would take precedence over anything on the outside.

The echo of the words "go with your gut" played in the back of her head during every date she went on, in the midst of every kiss she'd enjoyed, or not, even during post-coital conversation when she'd hear the phrase *I love you* and flick it away like an insect crawling up her leg.

When she got off the plane at LaGuardia after visiting her parents in Fort Lauderdale for Christmas, she requested an Uber. After ten minutes of waiting in front of the Delta terminal and cursing as the sun went down, she was about to request another car when a black limo pulled up right in front of her. The driver rolled down the passenger side window and smiled.

"Andrea Peterson?" he asked.

"Yes, but I didn't request a limo. I asked for — "

"I know, a compact. But tonight is your lucky night. I'm driving this car, and you get to relax in luxury."

She looked into his blue eyes, taking notice of the sorrow they exuded and tightened her grip on the handle of the suitcase.

"I'm sorry," she said. "I don't even know if you're legit. You're supposed to have a..." She glanced at the passenger side window and saw his decal. "Okay, you have the decal. But how do I know if — " He held up his phone and pointed to her name and phone number at the bottom of the screen.

"I told you, Andrea. Tonight's your lucky night. Plus, a woman like you *deserves* a limo, not a Honda Civic."

The driver pressed the button to open the trunk, got out of the car and walked over to Andi. He grabbed the handle of her suitcase and, before placing it in the trunk, asked, with only a look, if it was okay for him to drive her to her destination.

There was something so genuine about him that she was confident in her belief that he was who he said he was, so she offered a shy smile and nodded

"Great," he said. "We'll have you home in no time."

When they finally exited the maze of roadway leading out of the airport, he got onto Grand Central Parkway and was cruising at a good clip until brake lights appeared in front of him. He looked at the map on his phone's display.

"Shit," he said, looking in the rearview mirror. "I'm sorry. I shouldn't have said that. It's just... there's an accident up ahead and no way off the parkway until we pass it." He enlarged the visual on his screen. "It'll add about another ten minutes to the drive. Please help yourself to some Perrier. There are bottles in the side panel fridge. They should be nice and cold by now."

Andi opened the small refrigerator and pulled a bottle from the top shelf. After twisting off the cap, she took a swig and gazed out the window at Astoria Park beneath them. She could only make out shadows of people walking across the grassy park, as the sun had almost completely settled below the horizon. The lights outlining the Robert F. Kennedy Bridge shone like beacons in front of them, and she had to hold herself back from looking again at the driver, her intrigue trying to crawl its way past her defenses.

There was something about him that captivated her. He was a decent-looking guy. Not the handsome man's man she'd typically go out with, but attractive enough to hold her attention. He seemed confident, had a good sense of humor and had treated her like a queen since the moment they met, something she hadn't experienced in months, maybe even years.

But a limo driver? Really, Andi, is that the best you can do?

"I know my information is on the window," he said. "But my name is Rick. Can I ask where you're coming from? Did you get to go anywhere good?"

"Lauderdale," she took another gulp of the sparkling water. "My parents moved there about five years ago."

"You didn't want to move with them?"

"Why would I? I'm twenty-six. Would you want to go with *your* parents if they moved there?"

"My parents are dead," he said without a hint of emotion or sentiment.

Shit, she thought, that's *the sorrowful look.*

"I am *so* sorry," she said, almost choking on the water. "Sometimes I don't think and end up saying the dumbest things."

"It wasn't dumb, just not thought through," he said blamelessly. "Trust me, I'm used to it. When you're our age, people think your parents are alive and well. Which they *should* be. I'm sure your parents were happy to spend time with you, *and* you probably went to the beach, which was well worth the trip."

He was right. She spent most of her days laying under an umbrella at Lauderdale Beach or by the pool at her parent's condo complex. Even during the two days it rained, she enjoyed the respite from daily video meetings and endless texts from cohorts.

There were times on the beach she'd get a jolt in her stomach, dreading her return to the stress of her job and New York City itself. Even on the plane ride home, a twinge would come out of nowhere, and she'd place her hand on her stomach and try to calm it with a gentle rub.

And yet, right now, in the back seat of a luxury limo, she felt more relaxed than she had in days. At first she wasn't sure why, and then she glanced in the rearview mirror and caught Rick giving her a subtle wink. That's when she realized it was him, his tone of voice and tranquil vibe that was keeping her calm and unworried about what tomorrow's first day back at work would bring. Riding in this vehicle, traffic jam or not, was the pièce de résistance of her travels. And she only had Rick and happenstance to thank.

Ignoring her gut and allowing emotion to take over, Andi fell for a loving limo, Uber and taxi driver who treated her like gold. The honeymoon phase lasted throughout the summer, into fall and halfway through the winter before Rick started acting strangely.

He was now anxious, fidgety and jumped at the slightest sound, nowhere near the person she'd met that night at the airport, the man who made her feel like a queen. His disposition, once calm and serene, had made a complete one-eighty.

No matter how many times she asked or pleaded with him to open up and let her in, he refused.

"I'll be fine," he'd say. "Let me handle it. Give me another month or two and I'll be back to normal. I swear."

Although she wasn't fully convinced, she stuck with him. And then Kyle killed himself. The jarring sight of seeing him sprawled out on his bedroom carpet had left her shaken to the core. She assumed that if she was in such bad shape, Rick must be going through something a thousand times worse.

Sure, the two of them didn't talk much. Rick would even taunt Kyle or tease him just to get a reaction. But his suicide changed everything, and just thinking of Rick living in a place where a man killed himself was inconceivable to her. That's when she demanded he move in with her, and he eagerly agreed.

Now, curled up on her sofa, looking at torn, moldy moving boxes filling her dining area, her insides churned from the acute awareness of her mistake. While she was worried about how she had allowed herself to get into this situation, it troubled her even more that she would never be able to get out of it — especially after what she had done for him. If anyone found out that she had played any part in what he asked of her, she'd have a lot of explaining to do.

She took a deep breath to help calm down. *Think clearly,* she told herself. *There's no reason for anyone to suspect —*

The buzzer from the lobby intercom interrupted her thought. *Whew, let's hope it's the curtains.* She jumped up, ran to the wall intercom by the front door and pressed the TALK button.

"Just leave it there," she said. "I'll get it later."

As she walked away from the intercom, there was another buzz that almost made her jump out of her skin.

She pressed the TALK button again. "I told you, leave the package, and I'll — "

But before she could finish her sentence, the woman's voice, loud and garbled by static, bounced against the walls of her entry-way. And she didn't sound very happy.

* * *

Parsons pressed the intercom button next to the slot reading *4D—Peterson.* She waited barely two seconds before pressing it again, her patience thin from too many holes in her theories and open-ended lines and empty boxes on her whiteboard, questions without answers.

After an odd-sounding high-pitched tone and some static, a woman's voice passed through the speaker box on the wall. "Just leave it there. I'll get it later."

Parsons rolled her eyes. If the building had a camera, she'd be able to show her shield or ID. But it didn't. The only way to prove she wasn't a courier was to press the button for a third time and recite her detective speech.

So she pushed the button for the third time and waited for the attitude.

A tone, then static, then, "I told you, leave the package, and I'll —"

"Ms. Peterson, my name is Katy Parsons, and I am a detective with the New York City Police Department, Sixth Precinct. You can either come down and let me show you my identification or release the door lock, and I will come up and show you my ID."

A few seconds passed before the voice replied.

"I'll be right down," she said.

Parsons would rather have this conversation in Andi Peterson's apartment, where she'd be able to look around and possibly pick up clues that could help her close some holes. But now Andi was on her way down, and if she wanted to remain in the vestibule or the building entrance, she was concerned visitors, residents or even deliveries might get in the way of keeping the woman focused.

She peered through the glass door at the building's stairway. Within a minute, a pretty, slight-framed brunette with hair in a bob around her round face bounced down the stairs. She stopped at the vestibule door and studied Parsons's face. Parsons held her ID up against the glass. She didn't take it down until the young woman's lips moved.

"Okay, detective." Her voice came through slightly muffled. "How can I help you?"

Parsons's gut clenched. In her experience, the innocent were ready and willing to invite her in, some even offering her tea or coffee. Andi Peterson wasn't moving to open the door. So did she have something to hide? Something to do with Devlin?

There was no way Parsons was leaving this building without finding out.

"Can I come in?" she asked, glancing at the door lever, then back at the woman on the other side of the glass.

Andi rolled her eyes. "What's this about?"

Parsons saw the uneasiness behind the rude gesture, the wariness tightening the young woman's features. *What's her story? Why is she so angry and scared?*

"It's about Frank Devlin."

Andi's expression didn't change, but she turned the lever to let Parsons in.

As she entered, she glanced around the small lobby and looked up at the stairway. "Can we talk in your apartment, or did you want to chat here, where everyone can see and hear us?"

Andi crossed her arms. "Here is fine. I work from home and haven't had a chance to clean up yet. It's a mess."

"No need to worry about a mess. I think it's best if we go — "

"No," Andi interrupted, "I said right here is fine. So why exactly are you here?"

"He's dead," she blurted out.

"And?"

Parsons confined her astonishment behind a tight grimace. "Hmmm. Well, I was going to say I'm sorry, but it's obvious you don't really care. That, or you're a very good actress. What was your relationship with him?"

Andi glanced at the apartment door behind Parsons, not wanting to maintain eye contact for some reason. "I knew him before, you know, before the whole Dylan Wright thing happened."

"No, I don't know."

She hoped her feigned ignorance might encourage — or provoke — Andi to provide some facts voluntarily, but she didn't say a word.

"How did you meet him?" asked Parsons, tilting her head to have the woman look at her. It worked. Her face was expressionless. *She hides it well. . . just need to find out what the 'it' is.*

"He's more of my boyfriend's friend. They were friends first. I think they met a few years ago."

Andi took a breath, deeper than the last one. And her next was deeper still. Her arms remained crossed, her fingers now fidgeting, pushing deep into her biceps covered by the linty black sleeves of her T-shirt. She was getting nervous; the perfect time to start digging.

"Who's your boyfriend?"

"Rick."

"Rick who?"

"If you want to talk to Rick, you'll have to talk to Rick."

"Oh, trust me, Andi. He's next on my list. So if Rick no-last-name was friends with Frank Devlin, why did *you* visit him instead of Rick?" At Andi's startled glance, Parsons explained, "We saw your name on the visitor's log."

"He's too busy. He felt bad that Frank was all alone there. That's why he asked me to visit him."

"That sounds a little strange, Andrea."

Nothing.

"It sounds strange, *Andi*. And let me tell you why. Devlin murdered a fine young man. He's a *killer*, a *murderer*. And yet your *boyfriend* pities him and sends *you* to visit him in a psych ward. Were you at all scared for your safety?"

Andi shook her head, her fingers pressing deeper into her arms.

"I was in a psych ward, for God's sake, with security guards. What could happen there?"

"You'd be surprised," Parsons said, as dryly as if she was clearing her throat. "Now, what did you and Devlin talk about?"

Andi took a deep breath and released her arms, sliding her hands into the front pockets of her high-waisted ankle jeans.

"Nothing, really. Just what he does every day — not much — my job, Rick's job, things like that."

Parsons had something of the predator in her, and she knew it. The more anxiety Andi revealed, the more adrenaline flowed in Parsons's veins, pumped in her heart, sharpened her mind. She didn't like this woman — not her tone, her attitude, or the way she tried hiding her fear with confidence. Her behavior only pissed Parsons off more, making her want to go in for the kill early. Instead, she kept her voice steady, her excitement under control. *One step at a time. Get this right.*

"Do you know who you were talking to?" she asked.

"What do you mean, who I was talking to?"

"Well, you *do* know that Frank Devlin had multiple personalities, don't you?"

Andi looked to the floor. "Yeah, I know he does... did."

"So, who were you talking to?"

"Nathan," she said, sliding the toe of her blue Nike sneaker across the green and white tiled floor of the lobby.

"How do you know you were talking with Nathan?"

"I don't remember," she said, letting out a hard breath. She was trying to look annoyed instead of terrified, but Parsons sensed more fear. "Maybe he said his name or something. I just know it was him."

"Okay. You're in the psych unit at Bellevue, visiting a man I assume you've never met before, talking about your job and such, all because your boyfriend feels bad for him. And yet your *boyfriend* never visited him. He's not listed in any of the visitor logs. He never went to see Devlin before *or* after the day that you did. Don't you find that odd?"

"I told you before; Rick is busy. And I told him that the place was kinda creepy, and that stuff scares Rick. So... yeah... I think that's why he never went to visit him. He didn't want to get creeped out and have nightmares and shit."

Parsons took in every twitch and twinge the cornered woman attempted to hide with a sense of satisfaction. They were getting somewhere.

"And what does Rick do?"

"He drives people around. You know, like a taxi company, but he drives really nice cars, sometimes limos."

"Do you know if Rick ever spoke with Devlin after he went into the ward?"

"Not that I know of," she answered.

"Such a good friend, and he never talks to him?"

"He probably did. He just never mentioned it to me." Andi blinked, widening her eyes and forcing her scowl into a slight smile. "They're allowed to make calls on those pay phones in the ward. Maybe he used them to reach Rick."

"Or maybe he made phone calls with a cell phone that was given to him," Parsons said.

Andi crossed her arms again, her expression a combination of anger, loathing and panic. "I'm not a cop like you," she said, "But I've watched enough TV shows to know that I have the right to an attorney when we talk."

Smiling at Andi, Parsons stepped backward until she reached the far wall and rested her left foot against it. "Why would you think you need an attorney?"

"You're accusing me of something."

"What did I accuse you of?"

"Sneaking a phone to Frank." Andi's voice was getting louder and shakier with every word.

"I never accused you of anything. You're the one who seems to think you've done something wrong."

Andi slapped her thigh in frustration, which was probably also the source of the tears in her eyes. "That's why I need an attorney! I'm saying things I sh- can't- don't —" Andi's words became incomprehensible as she stumbled into chaos.

"Yes, you just might need an attorney. In the meantime, where is Rick now? Do you know?"

Andi looked at the tile, bouncing her heel off it as she shook her head without pause.

The problem was silence wouldn't help her now. Parsons wasn't leaving the building until she knew Rick's location.

"Where is he, Andi?"

Andi pressed her lips together so hard they slipped inside her mouth, leaving a thin slit.

"Okay, Ms. Peterson. You can either answer my question right here, right now, or I can bring you down to the station. Then we can get into a more in-depth discussion about you, your boyfriend with no last name and why you snuck a phone to Frank Devlin."

"Okay! Okay! Rick's at the shrink. He's had some issues, and we thought therapy might be a good thing for him."

"Issues? What kind of issues?"

"There is no way I'm going to talk to you about my boyfriend's therapy sessions. Now you're pushing it."

She let Andi settle down a bit and, in a very calm voice, filled with gentleness she didn't feel, said, "You're right. You don't have to tell me what his issues are. However, I can ask where he is at this moment. Do you know who his therapist is?"

She shook her head. "He doesn't want me to know. He thinks I'll call the shrink and try to get information about what they talk about. I told him I wouldn't, but he says he wants to keep things private until he's... well..." She used both hands to mimic air quotes. "... cured."

"Got it. Do you at least know where the therapist is located? It's important that I speak with Rick *tonight*."

"If you do that, he'll know I told you and never forgive me. He'll break up with me."

"Trust me, Andi. I'll make sure he doesn't find out you had anything to do with me finding him."

Andi folded her arms, her shoulders sinking in surrender. "I don't know exactly where it is. But I heard him talking to his boss on the phone this morning. He was going to pick up the limo so he could drive a client to somewhere in New Jersey. He said he'd be picking the client up just a block away from where he had to go for his appointment. Somewhere off Park, around East Fiftieth Street or Fifty First."

Feeling lightheaded, Parsons leaned her back against the wall. She closed her eyes and took a breath, making sure she wasn't letting her imagination run wild. After regaining her composure, she stood up straight.

"Andi, Justin Wright's office is off Park Avenue on East Fiftieth Street. Is Rick seeing Dr. Wright?"

"It can't be," Andi muttered, all her calm evaporating. She started pacing the lobby, even more agitated than Parsons had seen her yet. "Why Doctor Wright? Why would he see *him* after what Frank did to his son? How could he? No... it can't be that — "

"Andi!" Parsons's voice echoed through the hallway and up the stairs. She walked over to Andi and grabbed her by the arms. "Andi! Come on! Get your shit together here. You need to tell me what you know about Rick's issues. *Anything!* This could be a matter of life or death."

Tears streamed down Andi's cheeks, and her voice quivered through trembling lips. "I knew I shouldn't have gotten involved."

"Talk to me, Andi. Please. How long has he been in therapy?"

"It's only been a few weeks! He's been really angry lately. I mean, he's always been angry. Especially since... "

As she trailed off, Parsons's impatience boiled over. "Since what?" she shouted. "Is he angry with Dr. Wright?"

Andi shrugged.

"Is Dr. Wright in danger?"

Down the hallway, someone opened a door a crack, just wide enough to peek out at the source of the echoing words. At this point, Parsons didn't care if the entire borough heard her questions.

"I don't know!" Andi yelled back. "I didn't even know he was seeing Dr. Wright until just now. . . but I should have figured it out. He was really angry this morning. I thought he was going to hit me."

"Why today?"

"I don't know, but before he left, he said something about someone paying big for what they've done."

Parsons held her stomach as it twisted in a sudden bout of nausea. *This can't be. It just can't.*

"Do you think he was talking about his boss? The client he's driving? Dr. Wright?" she asked.

"I don't know! You're asking me questions I can't answer. Jesus Christ. I'm done. I have nothing else to say!"

Parsons restrained herself from slapping Andi across her face. "I tell you it could be life and death, and you tell me you have nothing else to say?"

Andi Peterson shrugged and shook her head vehemently. "I want an attorney. I'm not saying anything else."

Parsons headed for the exit. "You do what you gotta do. Just get down to the station on West Tenth, Sixth Precinct. I want you to wait there as long as you have to for me to show up. And yeah, I'd have an attorney with you," she added, pulling the door open. "A really good one."

She ran to her car. Once inside, she grabbed the radio mic and pressed the side button.

"This is Detective Katy Parsons. I have a possible 10-59 in progress at 126 East Fiftieth, first floor, office of Dr. Justin Wright. I need a car there immediately. Do you copy?"

"Yes. Copy. Will send a car there now."

"I'm on my way," she said, pressing her car's Start Engine button. "Don't wait for me to get there. Just make sure they get Dr. Wright to answer his door. Tell them to knock it down if they don't get a response."

"Copy that," she heard before throwing the mic on the passenger seat and turning on the siren and lightbar on the roof of her car.

She pressed her foot hard on the gas pedal and sped out into the street fast enough to hear tires screech.

"Not again," she whispered. "Please God, not again."

CHAPTER 20

Getting a parking spot right in front of Justin Wright's building was the only good thing to happen to Richard Davis since he'd woken up that morning.

The anger gnawed at his gut from the moment he opened his eyes, and he knew it wasn't going away; it would never go away. Not until he eliminated its source.

He took a shower, hoping it would wash off just some, even a few grains of the rage crawling over his skin. But it didn't work. Andi was on his ass about something to do with the electric bill, Paul was making him drive that bitch who lived on Fifty First all the way to New Jersey, and before he did that, he had to sit with Justin Wright and spew bullshit. Well, not anymore. Today the masquerade would end. He'd let his wrath see to that.

He looked at the cement path leading up to the building's glass entrance, the spot where he'd first met Nathan. Rick raked his fingers through his thinning hair as a vivid recollection of that day flashed into his head. He smirked, commending himself for using his ingenuity to make that "chance" encounter happen.

The week before it, there had been a truly chance encounter when his boss, Paul, called to give him a last-minute gig to pick up Justin Wright at his office and drive him home to Rye, New York.

"The *psychiatrist*, Justin Wright?" he asked.

"Yeah," Paul said. "Why? Do you know him?"

Wanting to hide any red flags, Richard chose his words carefully.

"I know *of* him," he said. "I've heard of him, yes."

"Good. Talk to him and see if he can help you become a nicer person." Paul cackled alone at his joke. Or was it a joke? "Just be waiting for him in front of 126 East Fiftieth at six o'clock."

Before he could reply, Paul had hung up.

Little did his wannabe comedian boss know, he'd thought about Justin Wright pretty much every single day for the past ten years.

With Justin in the back seat and the long ride to Rye in front of them, Richard Davis violated the limousine driver's number one rule: if your passenger is on the phone, don't eavesdrop on their conversation.

But this is different, Richard rationalized, *very different.*

From the tone of Justin's voice and the endearments he was using, Richard figured Justin was talking to his wife. Or his mistress, but he probably wouldn't discuss something so serious-sounding with a mistress. About halfway to their destination, he heard something that almost made him crash the limo into the car in front of him.

"You know how I feel, Mandy. It was the right thing to do at the time. Stephen was a reasonable threat to someone else, someone he

actually named, so I had to follow the rules and get the authorities involved. Needless to say. . . "

Richard tightened his grip on the steering wheel and took a deep breath. Justin's voice turned bitter, sarcastic.

"Well, the system did a great job, didn't they? Two days into the 72-hour hold at the psychiatric hospital, they found him hanging by a belt. That call I made really paid off, didn't it?"

Richard's stomach twinged. Beads of sweat dripped down his back, and he found it difficult to breathe. Then he heard something that proved exactly who Justin and his wife were talking about.

"You're right, Mandy. I'm sorry. Stephen Davis is not the issue right now. My new patient's problem is."

It was at that exact moment Richard Davis realized his constant anger wasn't an expression of hatred toward the entire human race. It was hatred of Justin Wright, the man who killed his father, a loathing that reached its turning point when he finally met the man in person, when he heard the indifferent tone in Wright's voice as he spoke about his father's death.

The screaming inside Richard's head was deafening. He no longer heard the whizzing din of passing cars, the car's tires hitting the road, or even the bullshit spewing from his passenger's mouth. He only heard his thoughts and their command to inflict harm on the person responsible for what happened to the only person he'd ever truly loved.

And that's when the commotion inside his head calmed, and he heard the echoing whisper of a single word: Avenge.

Seven days later, just before five o'clock, Richard stood in front of the door to Justin Wright's office building. He was waiting. . .

waiting to speak with the "new patient," the one he overheard described on Wright's phone call as someone with "split personalities." When he saw a young man slowly turn from the street toward the path to the front door, he started walking, head down, so he could purposely bump the man's shoulder.

"Oh, sorry, dude," Richard said. "I'm kinda out of it."

The man stopped and stared at him. And as he did, Richard could've sworn he saw the man's entire face change. It became thicker, as if he'd gulped in a mouthful of air, and his lips went razor-thin. His expression went from seemingly friendly to that of someone filled with as much rage as Richard.

Wow, this guy is weird.

Afraid the stranger was going to start an argument, maybe even punch him, Richard tried another apology. "I'm really sorry. How can I make it up to you?"

The young man took a breath and darted his eyes around the street as though someone had been chasing him.

"It's okay, man. I gotta go see this doc inside. He — "

"Dr. Wright?"

The man nodded.

"Yeah," Richard said. "I know him. Real shmuck." He waited for a reaction. The stranger didn't offer one, although at least his rage didn't visibly increase, either. "Sorry. I mean, if you like him, that's your business. I just think he's a shmuck."

The corners of the slit in the man's face rose ever so slightly until a smile finally appeared. A wave of relief passed through Richard's body. He was getting somewhere.

"I'm Nathan," the man said, holding out his hand.

"Richard," he responded. He took Nathan's hand and shook it with a tight grip.

"I think he's a shmuck, too," Nathan said. "Nothing but trouble."

"Then why are you here?" Richard asked. "Or is that too personal? Sorry... again."

"No, man, no. It's complicated."

Richard glanced at the front doors, then turned to Nathan. "Wanna ditch your meeting and get a scotch at Logan's?"

Nathan looked down at the pavement and then gave a mirthless laugh — at what, Richard hadn't a clue. *It's okay,* he thought; *the nuttier, the better.*

"Absolutely," he said. "Screw Justin Wright. Let's go."

Sitting at the bar, the two men clinked glasses before each taking a slug of Dewars.

"Ahhh..." Nathan sighed after swishing the scotch around his mouth. "Just what the doctor ordered!"

"Yeah," Richard said. "A *real* doctor. Not like Justin Wright!"

He hoped that egging Nathan on would get him some good information, maybe something important enough to help him carry out his plan.

"So, what did he do to *you*?" Nathan asked, circling the rim of the scotch glass with his index finger.

"Killed my father," Richard said without pause.

Nathan peered into his eyes. "What did you just say?"

"Okay, maybe he didn't kill him with his own bare hands, but he might as well have. My father was his patient. Wright threw him into the system without giving him the care he deserved."

"And what happened?"

"My father hung himself; that's what happened. If Wright had done his job and helped him instead of calling the police to take away my dad, he'd still be alive."

Nathan took a sloppy gulp of scotch and licked the excess off his thin, pinched lips. "Really sorry to hear that, dude. That just sucks. That's why I have to watch out for him now. He's trying to get rid of *me*."

"What do you mean?" Richard asked.

"Like I said, it's complicated. Too complicated to get into now. Let's just say he's trying to make me into *one* person, someone I don't want to be." He took another swig of liquor.

Richard nodded and feigned confusion. The research he'd done on split personalities and then, as he'd learned the terms, alters over the past few days gave him a good idea of what Nathan was referring to.

He took a lengthy glance around the room while waiting for the bartender to service customers at the other end of the bar. Once any observers were out of earshot, he tapped Nathan on the knee. When the man turned toward him, Richard pointed to his own ankle and lifted his pant leg high enough for Nathan to see the holster holding a .38 revolver.

"What the fuck?" Nathan asked.

"I carry it in case I have a passenger that goes cray cray on me. You never know these days." He let his pant leg fall. "I'm showing it to you because I have another one in the trunk of my car."

"I don't think I need one, I mean — "

"Like I said, you never know. And, I'm just saying, you don't want what happened to my father to happen to you. This will give you extra protection to make sure it doesn't."

Nathan kept his gaze on Richard's leg for a long time. When he finally looked up, he wore a smile from ear to ear.

"I could also use it to scare someone... if you know what I mean. I don't have to use it. Just waving it around might do the job."

"Exactly," Richard agreed, deep down hoping Nathan wouldn't settle for that. How nice would it be for someone else to take care of his business with Justin Wright? It felt like a dream coming true.

"Wow," Nathan said, gesturing for the bartender. "Today is my lucky day."

Richard laughed. "Mine, too," he said. "It couldn't have worked out better if it was planned!"

When he and Nathan met at Logan's again a week later, the first thing Richard did after sitting on the bar stool was pat his ankle.

"Do you have yours with you?" he asked.

"No, I keep it in my drawer, you know, the nightstand next to my bed. I only bring it out when I think I might need it. Tonight I'm hanging with you...." He took a swig of scotch. "Hopefully I won't need it." He grinned.

"Hopefully," Richard said, clinking his glass with Nathan's.

"By the way, did you know Wright's son has a gay roommate? The guy's name is Kyle. I wouldn't be surprised if Wright's son was a queer, too."

"How do you know about this guy?"

A bizarre look covered Nathan's face that made Richard wish he could take back the question.

He fidgeted, his features twitching as they began to transform. *This has to be because of one of his alters. I hope he's not changing to someone else.*

"I hear things," the man finally said. Richard recognized Nathan's voice and was glad no one had taken his place. "I also know that this guy Kyle was there the day Wright's son, Michael, was kidnapped. You heard about that, right?"

"Of course. Happened on the subway, didn't it? Tragedy couldn't have struck a nicer family."

"He was supposed to be watching him, and bam, next thing you know, the kid is gone."

"Really interesting," Richard said, feigning interest. It was time to get to the heart of the matter, *his* matter. "So, I've been trying to figure out how to get back at Justin Wright for what he did to my father, but I haven't come up with anything yet. Do you know how you're going to stop him from trying to get rid of you?"

With the crowd of Yankee fans across the bar screaming at the television, he didn't worry about his question being overheard by anyone else. Meanwhile, he was confident Nathan would understand him. One way or the other, he was going to get this guy to do his dirty work.

"Not yet, but..." Nathan stopped and swigged some more Dewars. "Nothing. Forget it."

"Hey, man," Richard said. "You can't start saying something, then say forget it. Now I *have* to know."

Nathan turned to him and leaned in close. "You have to promise... no, you have to *swear* to keep this quiet. If you don't, I *will* be using that gun you gave me."

"No worries, Nathan. A secret is a secret."

Nathan looked around the room, then met Richard's eyes again. "I've been visiting Michael Wright, you know, at the place he's being kept. I'm not getting into details, but I see him at least once a month."

Evil burned in Nathan's eyes, dripped with his words like invisible venom from the corners of his mouth.

"How the hell? What the fuck? You know where Wright's son is?" Richard asked, dumbfounded yet delighted.

"Shhh..." Nathan said above the screaming horde of fans. "I told you, no details. I was just telling you in case it gave you any ideas about how we can get Wright out of the picture."

Richard sipped some scotch and rubbed his chin. He'd think of something, for sure. The realization that he could destroy the entire family, not only Justin, almost brought tears of joy to his eyes. This was getting better by the minute.

"I have to think on it," he said, "but here's an idea off the top of my head. Tell the kid that Kyle, the gay guy, was involved in the abduction. That he actually *helped* the kidnapper take him away! That will really fuck with his head. And tell him other things. Like Kyle is screwing around with someone his father is trying to get rid of. That means Kyle is also putting his older brother's life in danger. Just play around with his head a little. It'll be great."

Nathan looked more confused than convinced. "Why should I do that? It's not the kid's fault his father's an asshole."

"And it wasn't *my* fault that Wright made my father hang himself. But I'm the one who suffered. I grew up without my dad, the one person in the world I looked up to. My mother lost the love of her life. So we all ended up grieving and suffering. Wright's family should suffer, too."

Nathan nodded slowly at first. As he thought more about what Richard said, his nodding sped up.

"I hear you, dude. You're right. Let's get back at all of them. You know that saying, 'The apple doesn't fall far from the tree.' It probably goes for them too. Father's an asshole apple; sons are asshole apples." He swirled his drink and waited until the ice stopped spinning. "Or something like that."

"Exactly, Nathan. I'm glad I found someone who thinks like me about Wright. Everyone else is all, 'He's the greatest,' 'He's the best psychiatrist in the country,' 'He helps so many people,' blah... blah... blah. That's bullshit. We know the truth. He's ruined my life, and now he's trying to ruin yours."

He held up his glass and waited for Nathan to do the same. After a silent toast and before he swigged the remaining scotch from his glass, Richard said, "We got this, buddy."

"Yes, we do!" Nathan cheered. "Yes, we do!"

Less than a month later, Dylan Wright was dead.

With Nathan now in Bellevue's psych unit, Richard had lost his only hope of taking care of Justin Wright *and* keeping his hands clean. Or had he?

He needed to get in touch with the man and make it clear where things stood. He couldn't risk being seen or signing in as a visitor. But no way could he call him on the ward's public pay phones — weren't those things monitored? A cell phone, then. A burner. And how to get it into Nathan's hands?

After he pleaded with Andi for three weeks to visit Nathan, swearing it only had to be "just once," she broke down, went to the hospital and snuck Nathan the phone. When she returned, she closed the apartment door, leaned her back up against it and uttered only five words to Richard: "Never again. Way too creepy." From there, she locked herself in the bathroom and took a two-hour bath.

The next thing on his list was to settle his living arrangements. A month earlier, he had been kicked out of his apartment for not paying his share of the rent. Andi took him in and told him he could stay there until he found a new place, but he hated the thought of going through the hassle of moving again.

One night, after a spontaneous hour of lovemaking on the sofa, Richard stroked Andi's hair where her head lay on his chest. *This is the perfect time to ask.*

"I've been staying here for a month already. Since we're practically living together, why not just make it permanent?"

Andi sat up and began the usual lecture — how they weren't ready, how she wanted it to be a mutual decision based on "desire" rather than "necessity."

"If we move in together now, it wouldn't be because it was the right time. It would be something that was forced. In the end, I'd probably resent you and blah... blah... blah..."

He'd drowned out the rest of her pointless babbling by trying to figure out ways he and Nathan could work together while the guy was in a loony bin.

Jesus, the timing couldn't be worse, he thought... until he realized it was perfect.

Dylan was gone, which meant Kyle would need a roommate. What better way to wreak more havoc in the life of Justin Wright than to move in with Kyle?

"Duh," he said to himself, nodding to Andi while still pretending to listen to her every word.

That night, he snuck out of bed and scanned the roommate search websites like a dog looking for its bone. After only fifteen minutes, he clenched his fist and held it up. "Yes!" he hissed, bringing the laptop up to eye level to make sure he was reading the words correctly: *Ask for Kyle*, with a phone number right beside it.

"Oh yeah, Kyle. I'll definitely be asking for *you!*"

Two weeks after Richard moved in, he and Andi were sitting on the sofa watching television when Kyle came home and, as he always did, walked directly to his room.

"He doesn't talk much, does he?" Andi asked.

"Other than 'Hello' and 'Goodbye' once in a while, the only other thing he's ever said to me was 'The rent is due on the first.'"

He turned up the TV volume extra loud, trying to goad Kyle, to get him angry enough to come out of his room and say something more. But Kyle didn't bite. He stayed in his room, door closed, evasion intact.

Andrea slapped Richard's arm and begged him to stop.

"That's not fair to him," she said. "He's just lonely and quiet. Why do you have to be so mean?"

"He doesn't know mean," Richard said. "Yet..."

And a few weeks later, he made good on his word. While Kyle took a shower, Richard donned a pair of Mr. Clean latex gloves, took a hard-cast bullet from his .38 revolver and put it in an envelope. He then took the red crayon he found in the back of his limo, probably dropped by that obnoxious Greenberg kid he drove to the airport earlier that morning, and wrote '*YOU KILLED DYLAN*' in a scrawl on a blank piece of paper. He folded the note, slid it into the envelope with the bullet and pushed it down into Kyle's bookbag.

Just as he heard the shower turn off, Richard threw the gloves back into the cabinet beneath the sink. He grabbed his phone and walked out the front door.

Halfway down the block, he dialed Nathan's number.

"Hey," Nathan answered.

"Hey, can you talk?"

"Yeah, I'm in my room."

"You're gonna love what I just did."

After telling Nathan about the bullet and note he'd planted, he held his breath, waiting for Nathan's response.

A few seconds later, Nathan said, "That's great shit, dude! I have to hand it to you."

Richard sucked up his accomplice's congratulations like a sponge.

"It really was a good idea," Nathan continued. "I just hope you're not wasting your time, you know, writing notes and shit."

"Just playing with his head a little. If it's a waste of time, it's a waste of time." Richard's high was falling fast.

"Well, here's something that's definitely *not* a waste of time," Nathan said. "How good are you at technology?"

"I picked up a thing or two. I actually learned Wordpress so I could write a blog about creating websites. But no one ever read it. I think I had like three followers."

"So you know your shit?"

"Depends. What are you thinking?"

"I'm trying to keep Kyle away from seeing Matthew. I did it once, but I know he'll be trying to see him again. One way to keep him away is to — "

"Wait, who's Matthew? Is he one of your... I mean... you know..."

"It doesn't matter who he is. That's not important. What *is* important is a video on a flash drive I have in my apartment. I need Kyle to see that video. Here's what I'm thinking... you buy a URL or domain name or whatever it's called. You upload the video there, then email Kyle, so when he clicks on the link, he'll watch it. Can you do that?"

"Not a problem," Richard said confidently. "By the way, it's called a domain."

"Okay, we'll call it a domain. But here's the catch. No one can find out who owns it *or* where the email came from. So once Kyle sees the video, the email address you use to send him the link and the domain both have to disappear... like they never existed. If you don't do that right, the cops will trace it back to you, me or both of us."

Walking up Eighth Avenue, Richard ran his free hand along a chain-link fence surrounding a construction site.

"That kind of shit involves things like purchasing a domain name anonymously, a separate encrypted email account, a VPN service and a lot of other stuff — including using cryptocurrency instead of traceable credit card info. I'm not sure I can..." He stopped walking. "Wait! What's your financial situation like?"

Nathan didn't answer.

"Did you hear me? Do you have any money?"

"Why?" he asked warily.

"I know this guy who's even better at this shit than I am. I *know* he can make sure no one finds out who did what. But I'm gonna have to pay him."

"How much?"

"A grand?"

Nathan huffed. "No problem. I actually have a load of cash hidden in a panel inside the guest closet in my apartment. I'm sure the cops were there after I was arrested and trashed the place, but there's no way they would have seen that panel. You and I are the only ones who know about it."

A jolt of electricity ran through Richard's veins. Euphoria overwhelmed him to the point that he had to restrain himself from jumping up and down. Screwing over one of Wright's friends, fucking over a weirdo roommate who treated him like shit *and* getting a thousand dollars! Things were looking up in a big way.

"Hold up a second," Richard said. "Where's your apartment and how the hell am I supposed to get in?"

"It's 106 Columbus on the corner of 106th. Apartment 4F. Down at the end of the hallway, there's a fire extinguisher. Open up the glass, and you'll see a piece of white tape along the bottom that blends in — you can barely see it. There's a key under the tape. It's an extra I keep there in case I ever lose mine."

"Wow, dude. You're rich *and* smart. You think of everything."

Nathan laughed. "Yeah, I do. And there are two more things you have to know before you do this."

Richard rolled his eyes. There was so much to do, a jumble of to-dos to keep track of in his mind, and he wanted this crap to be *done* already. "What are they?"

"One — make sure that after Kyle sees the video, you put the flash drive in his room somewhere. One of his desk drawers or something. And don't forget to wear gloves!"

"Easy enough." He hid how much it offended him that Nathan didn't think he was smart enough to know about the gloves on his own. "What's the other thing?"

"I want the domain name to be 'karmasuckskyle.com.'"

Richard jumped when his phone vibrated. He'd been so deep in thought; it took him a few seconds to realize where he was: sitting in the limo outside Justin Wright's office. The dashboard clock read 10:50. He had ten minutes before his session with his psychiatrist started. On the phone's display, Andi's name flashed and faded... flashed and faded.

He didn't want to answer it. She was probably calling to bitch about the boxes he hadn't yet unpacked at the apartment or remind him what brand of gluten-free bread he needed to bring home. This wasn't the time for either of those stupid conversations, though as his phone's display kept flashing her name, he was hit with a wave of guilt.

She'd helped him a lot over the past few months, stuck by him when he needed money or a place to live. She was even there when he opened the door to Kyle's bedroom and found him dead on the floor, empty pill bottles scattered all over the rug.

He'd called her over to the room and asked her to check his pulse, not wanting to leave a print anywhere in the room. Richard was stunned, never thinking his notes or that video he posted would make the guy kill himself. Sure, maybe he'd go a little cuckoo and need a shrink. But overdose on pills? He never imagined —

"Oh my God, Rick. He's dead!" Andi screamed. And then she started to cry, darting back from the body and seizing Richard's arm so tightly he thought his blood circulation might cut off. He pulled her out of Kyle's bedroom and into the living room, where he helped her sit on the sofa.

"Shhh... it's okay," he said, looking around the room for a sign that might tell him what to do next.

"Why would he...? What about his parents...? Did you have any idea...?" Andi spoke between sobs, wiping her tears and nose on her sleeve.

"No," he said, hugging her. "Not a clue."

"That's it. You can't stay here. You're going to move in with me."

He kissed her cheek and held her closer. Maybe those notes he left weren't such a waste of time after all.

Two days later, he got the call.

"Hey, Nathan. What's up?"

"I have a problem," Nathan said.

"Can it wait? I'm driving home from a gig so I can have dinner at a decent hour. Andi's waiting for me and — "

"I said I have a problem. Do we help each other or not?"

Richard made a right off Park onto East 83rd and pulled over in front of a fire hydrant.

"Sorry, dude. What's going on?"

"Justin Wright is what's going on," Nathan threw back as if he should already know.

"What are you talking about?"

"Wright's best friend, Dr. Bernard Malone, is a bigwig here at the hospital. He's gonna be a big part of the final decision about what happens to me. I overheard him talking to Wright on the phone. They're plotting to get me sent to some shithole insane asylum or crappy prison where they'll probably put me in solitary for the rest of my life."

"No freakin' way. They can't do that... can they?"

"These guys are doctors, wealthy shitheads who have connections. They can do whatever they want."

Richard watched the passersby, making sure none of them were cops who would bother him for parking in front of a hydrant. He kept his foot on the brake so anyone walking by would see his brake lights and assume he was getting ready to leave.

"What can I do?"

A few seconds passed before Nathan cleared his throat and sighed.

"There's really only one thing to do," he said. "Do you have that gun on you?"

Richard touched the holster on his right ankle. Over the past few days, he'd been driving through some dangerous areas in and outside the city, and the gun was doing its intended job — helping him feel safe.

"I have it with me, like always. Why?"

"When I was listening to Malone talking with Wright, he said he had a meeting tonight. Some divorce thing. That's where he probably is right now. I'm going to text you Malone's name, address and apartment number. I need you to wait for him there."

"How the hell did you get *that* information?"

"It's called a Google search... and a little snooping through files here. I have my ways."

"I'm sure you do." Richard's heart beat like a drum against his ribcage. He wasn't sure if it was fear, exhilaration or possibly pleasure. "Once I get him in the apartment, what do I do?" he asked.

"You need a step-by-step plan? C'mon, man. You either threaten the shit out of him so he'll keep me here until I can figure a way out, or you..."

Richard's heartbeat quickened. "Or I what?"

Another sigh. "Or you do what you gotta do. Just remember, don't leave any evidence. Not even a gun shell or bullet." He paused. "Do you hear what I'm saying, Richard? Can you handle this for me? Remember, I have a lot more money in the bank just waiting to be spent. Right now, *I* can't spend it, but *you* can. We don't have a lot of time. Just let me know now if you're gonna take care of this for me. We're in this together, remember?"

Nathan was right. They *were* in this together. The guy knew everything he'd done to Kyle. He also knew his plans to get back at Wright. If Richard didn't do what he was asking, the psycho would sing like a bird, and he could be in jail himself before the night was over. If he *did* do what Nathan asked, he'd be safe from Nathan's wrath, *and* he'd have some extra cash to spend.

"How much money are we talking?"

"How does fifty grand sound?"

Richard patted the holster on his ankle and slapped his leg.

"Text me the address!" he said before hanging up the phone.

Richard shifted the car into Park, unhooked his seatbelt and cracked open the windows. He removed his driver's sport coat, black tie and white button-down Van Heusen so he could feel the freedom that wearing only a T-shirt could provide. The bared skin of his arms breathed the outside air, and he rolled his shoulders to help loosen up some of the tension.

Smiling with anticipation of what the next few hours might bring, he wiped his sweaty palm on the white cotton tee Andi had cleaned the day before, along with the other fifteen or so other tees lying at the bottom of his hamper, the accumulation of his dirty clothing just another complaint in her arsenal.

Richard's phone started vibrating again, and again it was Andi. But his watch read 5:00. *Holy shit, I can't be late.* He took off his jacket and threw it over the buzzing phone. *Not now babe, I got bigger things to deal with. Much bigger things.*

He opened the limo door and placed both feet flat on the pavement. Before standing, he patted his right ankle to make sure everything was in place. *Nice and tight.* Of course, it always was — in the years he'd carried the gun, wearing the holster properly had become second nature — but now that the moment was approaching, he felt nervous and needed to double-check. *No worries... it's going to be okay.* He stood, slammed shut the driver's side door and locked it with his remote.

Walking up to the doors, Richard smiled as he passed the spot where he bumped into Nathan that fateful day. This time his head wasn't hanging down. He stood tall, eyes staring straight ahead, his mind focused on only one thing — destroying the source of anger that had been raging inside of him for the past ten years. Then, at last, he could find some peace. He could look at the people around him with indifference, maybe even warmth, something he hadn't felt in more than a decade.

CHAPTER 21

From the sun shining through the office window, Justin's desk lamp cast a shadow that resembled an old man, his head hanging low from the thinnest of necks. Despite the sunshine, Justin couldn't shake off a strange sense of darkness, of cold penetrating his skin, crawling so deep inside, he shivered and rubbed his arms to warm himself. For all his experience and expertise, he knew that any attempt to figure out what might be causing these feelings would be fruitless. Would he be able to unravel the mystery for a client sitting across from him? Probably. He always did. But now it was he who was sitting in the client's chair, and for the first time in decades, he was at a complete loss as to how he should handle the situation.

There was so much going on in his life; it would be impossible to pinpoint one specific issue anyway. And maybe that in itself was the cause of this dark feeling. Maybe he was juggling so many concerns and dealing with so many bizarre circumstances that his subconscious had to create physical symptoms, signs telling him to slow down and take a breath.

He had the situation with Michael to contend with. Had Mandy told Katy the truth after all? Or was their son more involved in the deaths of Kyle and Berny than she could accept? And God, how could Justin ever accept it if that was the case?

Then there was Jade. He'd been contemplating helping her remain in the psych unit rather than surrendering to the system where the poor woman would be thrown in prison for the rest of her life. Now, with Devlin's death and Jade's undeniable involvement, his request would be scoffed at by any attorney or prosecutor worth their salt.

And then there was his own grief and sorrow. He would have scolded any friend or family member who avoided their feelings the way he had. If he were his own patient, he'd have applied specific trauma reprocessing techniques to help understand and manage the effect of his losses over the past year. Dylan, Berny, and now Michael — the son he'd found but who still had a lot of demons and mental wounds to work through. He hadn't properly dealt with the anguish of these life blows and was now paying for it.

Gee, I can't imagine where this doom and gloom is coming from. His own sarcasm annoyed him. *God, it's time for me to see Van Sessler again.*

He looked at his watch. 5:01. Richard Davis was late for his appointment. What if he didn't show up? *Not such a bad thing,* he thought. It would give him some time to call Van Sessler and talk through a few —

Two loud knocks on the door.

"What the hell?" Justin whispered to the empty room. Richard knew there was a bell. He'd used it before.

Justin sighed and walked to the door. The moment he opened it, Richard barged in without even a "Good morning" or "Excuse me." He rushed to the chair he always used and sat down. Justin looked around the lobby outside his office door. A young, pretty, handsomely dressed Black woman was heading toward the elevator and smiled as she passed. He returned the smile and slowly closed the door. *At least there's one person who is in a good mood today.*

As he made his way to the chair opposite his patient, he started to speak. "Richard, you've always used the bell to — "

"This isn't working!" Richard barked. "I'm done with this therapy bullshit."

A sharp jolt ran up Justin's spine. Something must have happened to Richard on the way to his session, and Justin was about to get the brunt of it. He had to first calm himself down before trying to get Richard to do the same. After a deep inhale and a longer exhale, he sat back and crossed his legs.

"Richard, I have a feeling something's happened to upset you. Am I right?"

Richard sat glowering in the chair without a response.

"Okay, before we get into that, I just want to respond to your comments about this 'therapy bullshit' not working. Therapy doesn't work as quickly or as easily as most people wish it would. It takes time and a lot of work. We've only had three sessions. It takes longer than a few weeks to feel better when these feelings have been present for as long as you've had them."

Richard fidgeted and leaned his left elbow on the chair's arm. "Ten years, to be exact," he said, his voice gruff and rumbling with ire.

"Oh, so you *do* know when this started?" *Finally.* The sense of a breakthrough surged through Justin, giving him new energy. He leaned toward Richard. "I think we have something solid to work with. When you say ten years — "

Richard interrupted by slapping his palm down hard on his own knee.

"Yeah," he said. "I *do* know when it started. And so do you!"

Justin's energy turned to jittery nerves. He caught his fingertips tapping on the sides of the chair. *Okay.* It still might be a breakthrough if he could manage it right. He quickly eyed the door and then brought his gaze back to Richard.

"What do you mean?" he asked. "How could I possibly know?"

He braced himself, not sure he really wanted to hear what Richard's response would be, sensing a trap but knowing there was no way for either of them to go but onward.

Richard leaned forward, elbows on knees, and locked his eyes on Justin's.

"Does the name Stephen Davis ring a bell?"

Shocked numbness surged from Justin's feet to his head. He grabbed the arms of his chair and squeezed, his heart racing like a hummingbird's wings. *Holy shit,* Davis. *Richard Davis. Stephen Davis. What in God's name. . .*

"Yes," Justin stuttered. "Yes, it does."

"Do you remember the first time I came here, and you said I looked familiar?"

Justin could only find enough strength to nod.

"That's because last year, when you needed a car service, I was the driver. Yeah, you wanted Jimmy, but he was out sick. So I drove you to your fancy-schmancy house in Rye while you talked to your wife about Frank Devlin. You didn't say his name, of course. You're too smart for that. But you brought up my father's name. You know, the man you threw into the system so he could hang himself. Remember?"

A chaotic surge of jumbled images and words crashed against the walls of Justin's skull like waves against crumbling cliffs. Not knowing which thoughts to grab onto and which to release, he found himself unable to answer Richard's question.

Anger tightened Richard's vocal cords, making his voice hoarse as he spat out each word.

"Well, I dealt with it the best I could. *For ten years!* But when I heard you spewing that shit in the car, it... it... put me over the fucking edge!"

Beads of sweat dripped down the small of Justin's back. His head ached, and his stomach cramped with terror. The feeling was awful in its familiarity: his body was in the grip of the same fear that had held him the night Devlin met him in this office. The night he killed Dylan. The look in Richard's eyes told Justin that if he didn't respond, or at least attempt to influence the conversation, he wouldn't make it out of there alive.

"Richard, hold on for one second, please," he said before clearing his throat. "That case has haunted me for years. I tried to get your father — "

"Case?" Richard yelled. "He was a *case*? Actually, Doctor Wright, he was a human being. Flesh and blood. My father. A man you took away from me because you didn't want to be bothered."

"I know he was a person, Richard," Justin tried as hard as he could to keep his tone calm. "I know he was a human being, which is why I can understand where your anger is coming from. You blame me for — ”

“Yeah, I do,” Richard interrupted. “You’re where the anger started and has grown every single day since. I hate *you*. I hate the *system*. I hate *everyone* because the one person who meant anything to me killed himself without saying goodbye to his family!” Tears dripped down Richard’s cheeks, and his body shook. “To me! He never said goodbye to *me*!”

God, Justin wished he could think straight. Still, he had to keep trying to calm things down. If nothing else, because *he* couldn’t leave his family, Mandy and Michael, without a goodbye.

Not here, where they’d already lost Dylan. Not now. Not like this.

“I hear you, Richard. I do. I know that — ”

“You know shit, Doctor Bigwig Wright. Let’s see how much you know. . . ”

Justin clasped his hands, rubbing the sweat across each palm with his thumbs. It did nothing to prepare him for whatever sick probing Richard Davis was about to put him through. How could he sweat when he was so cold? Chilled to his bones, like a corpse in a morgue.

“Did you know I became friends with Devlin?” Richard stood and walked behind his own chair. He grabbed the high back and gripped it. “Yeah, I was able to meet up with him. I knew the guy was crazy. But actually? That was a good thing. It offered up the perfect way for me to get back at you. He told me. . . or I should specify, *Nathan* told me you were trying to get rid of him. That’s when I gave him a gun and told him to use it if he ever had to save himself.”

Justin turned to the empty patch of floor where, that night so many months ago, that night as vivid as if it happened just this moment, he'd cradled his son as Dylan died from Devlin's gunshot. Bleeding out from a bullet fired with *this* bastard's gift. In an instant, his anger surpassed his fear, and his face burned like he'd been set on fire.

"You son of a bitch!" Justin yelled, not even caring if he made the situation worse. "You gave that man a gun? He used it to kill my son, for God's sake! He didn't kill me, you idiot! He killed my son!"

Richard didn't change his position. His hand remained on the back of the chair. But his expression curved with a small yet distinct smirk that made Justin wish he had a gun hidden under his own seat cushion.

"I'm not concerned with *your* loss, doctor. Any more than you were concerned with mine. And here's more news for you: Nathan told me he paid a few visits to little Michael and his kidnapper. Even got to have some chats with him one on one. So I said he should tell your little boy that Kyle was involved in his kidnapping *and* that he was putting his older brother's life in danger. Mess around with the brat's head some because the Wrights just have it too easy, even when they're held hostage. Pretty smart, huh?"

Even as he seethed, Justin tried to make sense of things. "Kyle? How the hell do you know about Kyle?"

"Oh, poor Doctor Wright. My name is Richard. My friends call me Rick. Did Kyle ever mention a Rick to you?"

Justin's heart skipped a beat. He wished he'd spoken more to Kyle since Dylan's death. But yes, he remembered —

"Kyle's roommate? You're *that* Rick?"

Richard nodded and smiled with apparent pride. "Yes, sir. I'm Rick. The one and only. The one who put the bullet and note in Kyle's bookbag — and then threw them out, of course. I couldn't take the chance of getting caught."

A statement that didn't improve Justin's odds of surviving this encounter, but by now, he was too furious to care.

"I'm also the one who left him the note telling him to take all his pills." He let out a huff. "The guy was a loser anyway. No big loss."

"No big loss? He has parents!" Justin yelled. "People who loved him. You took him away from them!"

Richard kept talking as if he hadn't heard. "Now here's the best part! So I had Andi, my girlfriend, sneak a phone in to Nathan so we could stay in contact. That's how he told me where he hid the key to his apartment so I could get the video I sent Kyle. And then Nathan calls me one night. Tells me his shrink wants to put him away in prison. . . or make him spend the rest of his life in an old rotten psych ward somewhere."

Justin's stomach clenched as he remembered the plans he'd told Mandy and Carla about, how proud he'd been to find some way to ensure Dylan's death was avenged.

"I really didn't care until he told me the guy was a good friend of *yours*. Gives me his name and address. So I'm hiding at the end of the hallway until your buddy comes home. Good thing he's short and weak cause as he's opening the door to his apartment, I push my way in behind him." Richard laughed and rubbed his hands together. "I guess I don't need to give you the details about how *that* ended. I really tried to talk some sense into him, you know, about keeping Nathan where he was. But I could tell he was just yessing me to death. So I forced him onto his terrace. Really nice flowers and potted plants, by the way." He laughed again. "Nathan told me not to leave any evidence. Not even gun shells or bullets. So I led him to the terrace fence. I swear doc, I only pushed him a few inches, and then gravity took over. *Kerplunk!* No more problems for Nathan — well, he's still in the psych ward and facing trial, I guess, but whatever — and more importantly, another stab in the heart of my father's killer. And *I* was the one who gave Nathan the idea to tell you to thank Michael, just to add a little spice to the recipe. I'm sure *that* fucked you up pretty good, huh?"

It had. But now, a ripple of relief swept through Justin. Richard's admission meant that Michael *was* innocent. Mandy had been right all along. Their son had nothing to do with any of these things.

Maybe with the strength that relief gave him, Justin somehow managed to control his rage, staying seated in case any sudden movement would cause Richard to lunge at him first.

"But you see, Doctor Wright, even with all that, even knowing how much you suffered, it still wasn't enough to get rid of my anger. It's still brewed... gotten hotter... bubbled over like a pot of soup on the stove my mother would forget about. No, there's only one way to stop the anger. Just one way to get rid of the rage and frustration I feel every single day, thanks to you."

Justin rose from his chair as Richard bent down and pulled something out of — his sock? That brief puzzlement was swept aside when Richard lifted his hand over the back of the chair, revealing a gun.

"Only one way," Richard said, his voice now calm, his expression almost peaceful.

Willing all his body's strength into legs that wanted to turn into jelly, Justin ran for the door.

As he passed over the spot where Dylan had fallen, Richard screamed his name so loud it echoed throughout the room.

"WRIGHT!"

But Justin didn't turn around. He lunged toward the door, grabbed the knob, and as he was about to turn it, heard a loud familiar bang. And then another.

His legs wobbled, and then his head struck the wooden floor. Bringing his hand up to his neck, Justin felt warm liquid oozing. He was surprised at the lack of pain and how rapidly numbness was spreading throughout his body. His throat felt like it was swelling up, closing his airway.

He fought out a gasp and heard a soft gurgle with it. Was it from blood filling his throat? He tried taking another breath and heard the same liquid sloshing.

Behind him, another blast — the door? — and more gunfire. Yelling, unintelligible to him, muffled as if at a distance. The entire room, the entire world, seemed to be leaving him behind. Screams.

Warm strength cupped the back of his head, and soft skin brushed his cheeks.

It was the last sensation he could identify as everything continued to fade. Weightlessness enshrouded him, a gentle sense of calm. He listened to the blood pump with each heartbeat through the opening in his neck.

Through the haze of his dissolving vision, he saw Katy's face hovering over him. Anguish twisted it, and as if from a long distance away, Justin heard the sorrowful moan from her mouth.

Justin wanted to cry with her, grieve for them both, but his heavy eyelids fell down. Her weeping became silence.

His final thought was not about Katy, his killer or the reason behind what just happened. It was the hope that he'd see Dylan again — a hope that made him smile inside as a comforting warmth enveloped his body like the most snug of blankets, warmed by the sun itself.

CHAPTER 22

E verything was white.

A brilliant white, like the inside of a billowy, cumulus cloud infused with sunlight.

It was strange, Justin thought, the way he didn't have to turn around or use his eyes to see. The entirety of his surroundings was visible, perceptible without having to make the slightest effort.

Silence filled wherever he was, as did a sense of calm and serenity he couldn't remember ever experiencing before. Time seemed non-existent — no regrets of the past, no worries about the future. There was only now, and that was all he needed.

As he stood, floated, drifted — he wasn't quite sure — the surrounding white started breaking into minute particles, so tiny he was astonished that he could still see them. Another example of his strangely powerful perception here. The cloud thinned to a haze, to a vapor, that separated before him, atom by atom, until a familiar scene was revealed. Once the mist had fully cleared, he realized that what appeared in front of him wasn't somewhere *he'd* been before. It was a place Mandy had told him about, a place in a dream she'd had.

She said he'd been in it too, though not like this.

The memory of her words came to him like a cool breeze on a hot summer's day. . .

You and I were in the backyard. The trees were in full bloom, the garden brimming with the most vivid flowers I'd ever seen. I remember wondering who planted them because I knew I didn't. But honestly, within a few seconds, I didn't care. . . .

They were so beautiful, and their colors were so brilliant; I actually touched them to make sure they were real. The petals were soft as silk, so smooth and delicate; I almost cried at how beautiful they were. The grass so green it was almost emerald. . . .

And then I looked over at the giant maple, the one that Dylan and Michael had the tire hanging from. But there was no tire. No rope.

Just —

Dylan waited under the tree, just as she had seen him. But this time, there was a tire hanging from it, barely swaying in the whisper of a breeze. Pure love filled Justin's being as he made his way to his son, who was holding out his arms. Mandy had been right. He was more beautiful than the flowers in their brilliant colors. His face glowed with a perfect smile.

When Justin gently touched Dylan's face, his skin was warm and soft. He put his arms around his son and hugged him with the thought of never letting go. Time had truly vanished; it was all undone — Dylan running into his office, the gunshot, the look of fear on Dylan's face as he took his last breath. It had happened. But here they were, all the same.

He was about to say his first words to Dylan when he heard a strange beeping sound. Behind him? Above him? Whatever it might be and wherever it was coming from, the noise wasn't stopping.

Beep... beep... beep. He looked at Dylan, hoping for an explanation. Neither of them had yet uttered a syllable.

And then the softest whisper filled the air.

"You stay with me, Justin," Mandy's voice said. Though quiet, he heard her determination. *"You will not leave me, and you will not leave Michael. We need you here."*

Here? Where was —

He no longer had Dylan in his arms. Instead, Justin sensed his own body — an almost suffocating confinement after where and what he had been. Gravity pulled at him. He was lying down — *a bed, I think* — as warmth washed against his ear. He recognized the rhythm of Mandy's breath. Beyond her, there were voices he didn't recognize, but a sound he did: *beep... beep... beep*. A monitor in the room, tracking, he knew, his vital signs. He didn't like it. He didn't like anything about this place other than Mandy's voice and the touch of her hand in his. He wanted to return to where he'd been.

He numbed his mind, pushing away any thoughts or images other than those of Dylan and the place where they had just been reunited.

Back in the yard, his son stood waiting. He met him in the middle of the lawn and kissed him on the cheek.

There was no need to speak. He asked his questions without opening his mouth, a body part he wasn't sure even existed here.

"Is this real? Or is my mind playing tricks on me? Am I hallucinating? Am I dying?" He held Dylan's gaze. "Do you know?"

His son kissed him on the cheek and gave Justin a smile that warmed his soul. That smile didn't move, although he heard Dylan's voice saying,

"Only you know."

"What do you mean? Dylan?"

Somehow there was space between them again. Justin tried to step toward his son, only to pass through what felt like a screen, a mesh of particles. He tried grabbing onto something, anything that might stop him from being pulled backward. But there was nothing his hands could reach, nothing around him except empty space — brilliantly white space with a radiance of tranquility that eventually stopped his desperate grasping, relieving his worry enough that he allowed himself to be taken.

"I know you can hear me," he heard Mandy whisper. "I'm staying right here until you wake up."

She still held his hand, rubbing a finger into his palm. But this time, he felt something in his other hand. He tried to speak, but something was lodged deep in his throat. He barely had the strength to make a sound, let alone move a muscle.

A soft, warm breath on the lobe of his other ear and then a voice.

"I'm here too, Dad. Mom and I want to be here when you open your eyes. If you can squeeze my hand, please try."

But Justin couldn't. He was too weak, dizzy, floating in and out of two different states of consciousness that left him bewildered. What was real? What wasn't? Were Mandy and Michael really whispering to him? Was he just imagining Dylan standing before him?

Something warm dripped from his eye and down the side of his face. It tickled until a touch wiped it away, and he felt something pat the wet spot.

"It's okay, honey. I love you," he heard whispered in one ear.

"I love you, too," he heard in the other.

And then, a gust of air pulled him through the brilliance and back into the yard, where Dylan sat on the tire hanging from the giant maple.

Justin walked to him and sat down on the grass, green as emerald, smooth as silk. He touched his son's bare feet with his fingertips, remembering them as they were when he was a baby, the toes Justin had nibbled to make him laugh. Looking up at his son's face, he waited for him to speak.

But Dylan didn't say a word. Instead, he looked back at his father as though waiting for an answer to a question he hadn't asked.

Justin locked eyes with what he could only imagine was an apparition, a hallucination brought about by trauma, medication or a fantasy so desired that madness had finally won.

"Don't doubt yourself," Dylan said. "*Everything* is real."

Again, it was more like thought than speech. But either way, it was a conversation with Dylan. "I like it here," Justin said in his mind. "I feel safe. I feel at home."

Beep. Beep. Beep.

"Do you want to stay?"

I love you, Justin.

Justin didn't answer — unable to even think of his answer.

"I know, Dad. I know. But it's a decision only *you* can make."

Justin kept his eyes on Dylan's. "When do I have to decide?"

Stay with me, babe. Michael and I are right here waiting for you.

Dylan smiled and tilted his head, turning upward as if to better hear the voices in the distance.

"Now," he said. "Now."

I'D LOVE TO HEAR YOUR THOUGHTS ABOUT "AVENGED"!
If you'd like, send me an email at:
Rob@RobKaufmanBooks.com

Other books by Rob Kaufman

One Last Lie
A Broken Reality
The Final Step
The Perfect Ending
In the Shadow of Stone

JUSTIN WRIGHT SUSPENSE SERIES

Altered
Jaded
Avenged

Scared
(coming in January 2024)

Milton Keynes UK
Ingram Content Group UK Ltd.
UKHW020921201123
432908UK00020B/2688

9 798223 016502